MARRIED FOR THE TYCOON'S EMPIRE

BY

ABBY GREEN

MILLS & BOON

First published in Great Britain 2016
By Mills & Boon, an imprint of HarperCollins*Publishers*
1 London Bridge Street, London, SE1 9GF

Large Print edition 2017

© 2016 Harlequin Books S.A.

Special thanks and acknowledgement are given to
Abby Green for her contribution to the Brides for
Billionaires series.

ISBN: 978-0-263-07058-3

Our policy is to use papers that are natural, renewable
and recyclable products and made from wood grown in
sustainable forests. The logging and manufacturing processes
conform to the legal environmental regulations of the
country of origin.

Printed and bound in Great Britain
by CPI Antony Rowe, Chippenham, Wiltshire

MARRIED FOR THE TYCOON'S EMPIRE

I'd like to dedicate this book
to the Mills & Boon authors who inspired
me from the very beginning: Susan Napier,
Emma Darcy, Robyn Donald, Sara Craven,
Helen Bianchin, Penny Jordan,
Sally Wentworth, Sara Wood, Kate Proctor
and Stacy Absalom, whose book
Ishbel's Party is still my touchstone for
the high-stakes high emotion these books
promise. Thank you!

PROLOGUE

BENJAMIN CARTER SAT in a high-backed leather chair in a corner of the private members-only club. The lighting was artfully dim, and the atmosphere was hushed and exclusive. Warm golden lights and flickering candles added to the sense of rarefied privacy. Cigar smoke curled into the air from another dark corner, adding an exotic aroma and diffusing the light.

The club promised absolute discretion, which was specifically why he'd chosen it. And now Ben looked, one by one, at each of the other three men who had joined him at his table. At his request.

Sheikh Zayn Al-Ghamdi—the ruler of a desert kingdom rich in oil and minerals, whose wealth was astonishing and control absolute.

Dante Mancini—an Italian renewable energies mogul whose charming, handsome exterior hid a rapier-sharp intellect, business acumen and a sarcastic tongue that could strip paint from a wall—as Ben had discovered during one particularly acrimonious deal years before. Right now he wasn't exuding charm; he was glowering darkly in Ben's direction.

And, last but not least, Xander Trakas—the Greek billionaire CEO of a global luxury goods conglomerate. He was cool and aloof, with strong features that gave nothing away. Ben had once told him grudgingly that he should play poker if he ever lost his vast fortune and needed to win it back. Which was about as likely as a snowstorm in hell.

Ben might not rule over a desert kingdom, or half of Europe, but he ruled over Manhattan with his towering cranes and the deep pits he forged out of the ground in order to build new and impossibly ambitious buildings.

The tension around the table was palpable. These men had been his nemeses for so long—and each other's—that it was truly surreal to be sitting here now. What had started out as minor infractions during various deals over the years had escalated into entrenched warfare, with each recognising in the others formidable adversaries to be defeated and vanquished. The only problem being that each one was as successfully ruthless and stubborn as the other, so all they'd ever achieved was a series of tense stalemates.

Ben sensed that Dante Mancini in particular was about ready to bolt, so he sat forward. It was time to talk.

'Thank you all for coming here.'

Sheikh Zayn Al-Ghamdi's dark eyes were hard. 'I don't appreciate being summoned like a recalcitrant child, Carter.'

'And yet,' Ben pointed out, 'you're here.' He looked around. 'You all are.'

Dante Mancini drawled, 'And the prize for stating the obvious goes to Benjamin Carter.' He lifted his heavy crystal glass in Ben's direction and the dark liquid inside shimmered with golden opulence, reflecting the decadent luxury of the club around them. He downed his drink in one and simultaneously gestured for the waiter. He caught Ben's look. 'Tempted to drink something stronger than *water*, Carter?'

Ben fought down the urge to rise to Dante's jibe. He was the only one of them not indulging in the finest single malt whisky one could buy outside of Ireland and Scotland.

He looked pointedly at the others. 'Gentlemen, as fun as it's been over the last decade, squaring up to each of you, I think you'll agree that the time has come for us to stop giving the press an excuse to pit us against each other.'

Xander Trakas looked from Ben to the other men and sighed. 'He's right. The press have targeted us all, one by one, and what started out as a few salacious gossipy pieces in that rag *Celebrity Spy!* have turned into something much more serious. While I believe we're responsible for the stories that end up in those rags due to our own lax PR, I draw the line at spurious claims of excessive partying, revolving bedroom doors and, most damaging of all, conspicuous absences at the office.'

The Greek tycoon's face hardened with displeasure. 'The fact that I've been pulling all-nighters in the office when they say I'm out partying is infuriating. I lost out on a lucrative contract last week because of doubts about my competence. It's gone too far.'

Dante Mancini made a sound of grudging agreement. '*I'm* about to lose out on a deal because they want someone with "family values"—whatever that is.' He took a healthy sip of his refreshed drink.

The fact that Dante Mancini and Xander Trakas were still here and agreeing with each other told Ben more effectively than anything that he'd done the right thing in asking them here this evening—and also that they had a very real threat on their hands.

He said, 'We're being reduced to caricatures, and these exaggerations of our private exploits are becoming too damaging to ignore. I can handle walking onto my construction sites and having my men rib me about a kiss and tell, but when gossip and innuendo starts to affect share prices and my professional reputation that's unacceptable.'

Trakas looked at him and there was an unmistakable gleam of mockery in his eyes. 'You're not trying to imply that your ex-lover made it all up, Carter, are you?'

Memories of lurid headlines—*The hard man of construction is just as hard in bed!*—made Ben snap back, 'Her story was as real as *your* infamous little black book that divulges the names and numbers of most of the world's most beautiful women. What was it they said, Trakas? Still waters run deep?'

Trakas scowled and Mancini scoffed, 'As if Trakas has the monopoly on the most beautiful women. Everyone knows that I—'

A cool voice cut them off, 'If we're quite finished with the dissing contest, perhaps we can discuss how to get ourselves out of this mess. I agree with Carter: it's gone too far. This adverse attention is not only affecting confidence in my leadership, but also my business concerns. It's even affecting my little sister's chances of the marriage she wants, and that is unacceptable.'

They all looked at Sheikh Zayn Al-Ghamdi, who had sat forward. The dim lighting made the lines of his boldly handsome face stand out harshly. They were all dressed in classic black tuxedos except for Mancini, who was bucking the trend in a white jacket with his bow tie rakishly undone.

It reminded Ben of the function they'd just come from and he said grimly, 'It's not just our business concerns...or our families.'

Mancini sat forward too, frowning. 'What do you mean?'

Ben glanced at him, and at the others. 'The director of the charity came to me this evening and told me that if this media furore doesn't disappear she'll have to remove us all as patrons. She's noticed an adverse effect, with less tickets sold and people not showing up.'

Dante Mancini cursed colourfully in Italian.

The Sheikh said ruminatively, 'So that's why you asked us to come and meet you?'

Ben nodded. 'I think we can all agree that the last thing we want is for the charity to suffer because of us.'

The charity in question was the only thing that linked them all, outside of pitting their wits against each other during business deals, and its function was the only time of year when they were all in the same room at the same time, which invariably caused much media interest.

The Hope Foundation focused on giving funds to young kids—girls and boys who were from disadvantaged backgrounds and showed an aptitude for business and enterprise.

Dante said now, 'Carter's right. We can't bring the charity into this mess.'

For the first time Ben had to recognise a sense

of kinship. They all genuinely cared about the same thing, and it was slightly disconcerting when he'd depended solely on himself for so long. It wasn't entirely unwelcome—almost as if a burden had suddenly been lightened.

And then Sheikh Zayn's cool voice said, 'So what the hell is the solution?'

Ben looked at him, and glanced at the others. 'I'm guessing that, like me, you've consulted with your legal teams and realised that it isn't worth the added publicity to sue *Celebrity Spy!*?'

They all nodded.

Ben went on, his voice as grim as the faces around him. 'Issuing a statement will also get us nowhere; we've gone beyond that point. If we do that it'll look like we're backtracking, trying to defend ourselves.' He sighed volubly. 'The only solution is for us to be seen to be cleaning up our acts—comprehensively and for the long term. Unless we do, I don't think it's going to go away. If anything, they'll only start to dig deeper, and I can assure you that I for one have no desire to invite further scrutiny.'

Dante's gaze narrowed on Ben. 'You don't want

people being reminded that your rags to riches story isn't entirely accurate?'

Ben's whole body tensed and he glared at the man. 'I've never hidden my origins, Mancini. Let's just say I've no desire to have old history raked over again. Just as I'm sure you'd prefer not to invite a spotlight onto your own family background?'

Ben was referring to the way Dante was so zealous about guarding his family's privacy—which could only mean he had something to hide.

After a tense moment the ghost of a hard smile touched Dante's mouth and he lifted his almost empty glass in the air. '*Touché*, Carter.'

Sheikh Zayn interrupted tautly, 'I think we can all appreciate not wanting to attract even more attention, for whatever reasons we may have.'

Ben was aware of Xander Trakas shifting uncomfortably to his right, evidently ruminating on the skeletons in his own closet.

A brooding silence descended on the group for a moment and then the Sheikh said with a grimace, 'I agree with Carter that cleaning up our personal lives seems to be the only viable solution. As much as I've tried to avoid it, I know the only thing that will restore my people's faith in me will be a strategic marriage and producing an heir to the throne.'

Ben was aware of the collective shudder that seemed to go through all of them. With the utmost reluctance, he had to admit, 'After discussions with my PR advisor and my solicitor, I've come to a similar conclusion.'

Dante said, with evident horror, '*Marriage?* Do we really need to take such drastic action?'

Ben looked at him. 'Even I can see the benefit in marrying someone suitable. It will restore confidence and get the press off our backs. It'll also restore trust. I've found myself in numerous social situations where clients' wives have made their interest all too obvious, much to the anger of their spouses. It's only a matter of time before a deal falls through because of petty jealousy—or, worse, the belief that something happened.' Ben looked around the other men. 'We're being seen as threats, in more ways than one. And that's not good.'

Dante's irritation was obvious. 'You said someone suitable—what is *suitable*? Is there such a woman?'

Sheikh Zayn answered, with all the confidence of a man who came from a society where arranged marriages were commonplace. 'Of course there is. A woman who is happy to complement your life... a woman who will be discreet and loyal above all.'

Dante raised a brow. 'So, genius, where do we find this paragon of virtue?'

For a moment there was silence, and Ben tensed again, suspecting that Dante Mancini had gone too far. Sheikh Zayn was a head of state, and used to far more reverential exchanges.

But then the Sheikh threw his head back and laughed, long and hard. When he looked at them all again he said, 'Do you know how refreshing it is when someone speaks to me like this?'

The tension that had been pulled taut between them ever since they'd all sat down seemed to relax perceptibly.

Dante smiled and gestured with his glass towards the Sheikh. 'If you would finally agree to discuss alternative energies with me, I'll disrespect you as much as you want.'

Sheikh Zayn's eyes flashed with rare humour. 'Now, *that* is an offer I could consider.'

Ben cut in. 'As warm and fuzzy as this cessation in hostilities is, we need to focus on the fact that we've agreed that promoting a more settled front is the way to deal with this situation. And for that we need to find women who are happy to marry us quickly and conveniently. As Sheikh Zayn said, women we can trust, who will be discreet. Loyal.'

Dante Mancini's smile faded and he said darkly, 'You'd have more luck finding a leprechaun riding a unicorn down Fifth Avenue.'

They contemplated that silently for a few seconds, and then Xander Trakas said quietly, 'I know someone.'

They all looked at the man who, Ben realised, had been suspiciously quiet up till now. 'Who?' he asked, intrigued.

'A woman. She runs a very discreet dating agency aimed specifically at people like us. She knows our world inside out—'

'Who is she to you?' cut in Dante. 'An ex-lover?'

Xander glared at him, not looking so aloof now. 'That's none of your business, Mancini. Just trust me when I say that if anyone can set us up with the right women, she can.'

The Italian mogul held up a hand. 'Fine—keep your pants on.'

Ben, who'd been absorbing all this, looked to Sheikh Zayn. 'Well?'

The Sheikh looked as if he'd prefer to sign up to a knitting class, but he finally said heavily, 'I think it might be the best option… If we're doing this, time is of the essence—for all of us.' He punctuated that with an expressive look at each of them.

Dante eventually said, with palpable reluctance, 'Fine. I'll take her details but I'm not promising anything.'

Ben held out his phone to Xander Trakas and tried to ignore the sensation of his collar tightening around his neck. 'Put her number in there. I'll call her next week.'

As Xander added the contact details to Ben's phone Sheikh Zayn sat forward and said, with another glimmer of wry humour, 'Do you know, I've actually forgotten what it was that set us off against each other in the first place…?'

Ben quirked a rueful smile. 'I think we have to admit that perhaps we liked being adversaries too much to give it up.'

Xander put Ben's phone down on the table. He held up his glass. 'Well, then, maybe it's time to concede a mutual defeat for the benefit of a bigger victory. Restoring faith in our reputations, which in turn will restore confidence in our businesses and profit margins. Because, as we all know, that's what's most important.'

Dante Mancini lifted his glass and drawled, 'Hear, hear. To the start of a beautiful friendship, gentlemen.'

Ben looked around at each of the men and thought that in spite of the slightly mocking tone of Mancini's words something *had* shifted here tonight. These men were not foes any more. They were allies and, yes, possibly even friends.

Ben raised his glass to join the others. Nothing was going to get in their way now. Not even the women they would take as their convenient wives.

CHAPTER ONE

BEN CARTER STOOD near the main window in his office, with its impressive views over downtown Manhattan. The thing that usually pleased him most when he took in this view was seeing his construction cranes high in the sky, dotted around the island. Right now, though, he had his back to the view and every line of his body was in defence mode, from his crossed arms to his tense stance.

'So, I think that about covers it.'

He bit back the urge to ask snarkily if she wanted to know what colour underwear he was wearing today.

The woman seated by his desk glanced at him and observed wryly, 'You don't like answering personal questions, do you?'

Ben bared his teeth in a forced smile. 'What-ever gave you that impression?'

Elizabeth Young, the matchmaker, shrugged nonchalantly as she tapped something into her palm tablet. 'I think the fact that you look about ready to jump out of the window gives it away.'

Ben scowled and walked back over to his desk. With every question she'd asked—from innocuous ones like, *What's your favourite holiday destination?* to more edgy ones like *What is it you want from a relationship?*—he'd put more and more space between them. As much as he recognised his need for a convenient wife, the quantum leap from a life of no-strings encounters with beautiful women to a committed relationship— albeit for convenience's sake—was making Ben's skin prickle uncomfortably.

After witnessing the collapse of his parents' marriage, which had fallen like a deck of cards at the first sign of trouble, Ben had never entertained notions of domestic bliss.

The matchmaker was right: if he could have jumped from the window he might just have tried it.

He scowled harder as he sat down—who the hell's idea had this been again? *Xander Trakas.* Recalling the Greek man's reaction that night, when Mancini had asked if this woman was an ex-lover, made Ben assess the slim and elegant blonde on the other side of his desk.

Hair that looked as if it tended towards being curly was tied back in a low bun. She was casually dressed, yet smart, in tailored trousers and a loose unstructured top under a fitted soft leather jacket. She oozed elegant style and, he had to admit, discretion and professionalism. Xander had been right.

As she looked at him now, he noticed that her eyes were an unusual shade of amber. Ben waited a beat to see if he had any reaction to her on a physical level. *Nothing.* He told himself that was good—the last thing he needed now was the distraction of someone he actually desired. Which brought him neatly back to why she was here.

He said, 'So, now that you've mined my soul for every tiny detail, who do you suggest is my best prospect for a partner?'

He saw the unmistakable flash of cynicism in her eyes, and a small smile tipped up her mouth at one side.

'Oh, don't worry,' Elizabeth said. 'I'm under no illusions. I know that you've told me only as much as you want to reveal. I know men like you, Mr Carter, that's why I'm good at my job.'

Ben decided to ignore the urge to ask exactly what she meant about knowing *men like him*. If it helped him to achieve what he needed to survive this crisis then what of it? He steepled his hands under his chin and admitted to a grudging respect for the way she wasn't intimidated by him, as so many were.

'Xander Trakas recommended you.'

And just like that this woman's composure slipped slightly, just as Xander's had that night in the bar, almost a week ago. She wasn't so sanguine now.

She avoided Ben's eye, fussing with the tablet. 'I have lots of connections, he's just one of them.'

Ben was intrigued by the button he'd obviously just pushed, but not intrigued enough to lose sight of his own goal. He became businesslike and sat forward again. 'Forget I mentioned it. So, do you have anyone specific in mind?'

She turned her tablet around to face him, laying it flat on the desk, and pushed it towards him. 'There are some possibilities here. Look through them and see if anyone piques your interest.'

Ben took the tablet and did as she had bid, scrolling through the pictures of women along with a few lines of their bios. They were all stunning in their own ways, and obviously accomplished. He scrolled past a human rights lawyer, the CEO of a software company, a UN interpreter, a supermodel...but none of them jumped out at him. He was about to hand the device back when one last woman appeared on the screen and something inside him went very still.

He didn't even look at her bio. He was transfixed by her. In the picture her shoulder-length dark brown hair was being blown around her shoulders and face by a breeze and she was laughing into the camera, revealing two dimples. She had high cheekbones and a lush mouth. He couldn't recall the last time he'd noticed dimples on a woman. Dark blue eyes, long-lashed. She was innocent and sensual all at once. And exquisitely, vibrantly beautiful.

For a second Ben found it hard to breathe. He also had a sense that she was somehow familiar.

Elizabeth obviously sensed his interest. 'Ah, that's Julianna Ford. Stunning, isn't she? She's British, and based in London, so that could prove a bit of a challenge, but as luck would have it she's actually in New York this week for a charity benefit.'

Ben frowned sharply and looked up. '*Ford*? As in Louis Ford's daughter?'

Elizabeth cocked her head. 'Do you know her?'

He glanced at her picture again before pushing the tablet back towards Elizabeth. 'I know *of* her. I met with her father a few years ago. I tried to persuade him to sell his business to me. He spoke of her, and I saw her pictures around his house, but she wasn't there at the time.'

Ben struggled to remember. She'd been away on holiday…skiing? Whatever her father had said about her, it had reinforced the impression he'd formed of her at the time: she was the spoiled and pampered only daughter of a doting billionaire father.

Ben had experienced that scene while in London, where the rich partied alongside royalty and to excess. He'd hated it. It had been a forcible reminder of the fact that if his father hadn't been so corrupt Ben would have still been part of that world too. Still living a blinkered life, blind to harsh reality. The harsh reality that had reshaped him into the man he was today. Answerable to no one and with his astronomical success bedded so firmly into the earth that he would never suffer the same fate as his parents—being at the mercy of volatile markets with no solid investments to speak of.

Ben diverted his mind from old and painful memories and focused on the matchmaker. And the future. Not the past. What she was handing him here was an opportunity not to be missed. The Ford construction company, with its solid black font signage against a dark green background, was a ubiquitous sight on construction hoardings in Britain.

Ben knew what a coup it would be to gain a foothold in Europe by acquiring one of its most respected companies—which was why he'd gone after it once before. Louis Ford had resisted his advances then, in spite of his rumoured ill health, but Ben had been keeping an eye on him ever since, and he realised now that Ford had gone quiet in recent months. *Very* quiet.

And now the man's daughter was here. Looking for a date.

Suddenly Ben realised that Julianna Ford represented the solution to all his problems. If he was to take the drastic step of committing to one woman for the sake of his reputation and business, then why not pursue a marriage that came with solid potential for business expansion? If she agreed to marry him Ben's empire would extend into Europe and he would have reached the very pinnacle of everything he'd set out to achieve. All with a stunningly beautiful wife by his side.

He looked at Elizabeth and a sense of delicious anticipation coiled through his gut. He said, 'She's the one I want to meet. You can set up the date.'

Lia Ford was trying to curb her mounting anger, but it was hard. Her stiletto heels clacked sharply along the wide Manhattan pavement, as if to underscore her volatile mood.

First she was angry with her father for his meddling ways, even if his heart *was* in the right place. And then she was angry with her father's secretary, for following her father's instructions to give all of Lia's information to Leviathan Solutions. She was even angry about the photo that had been given to the agency—one her father had taken, catching Lia off-guard during a happy sailing trip. A far too personal memento for a dating website!

As the Leviathan agency's global operations were based in New York, Lia had gone to Elizabeth Young's Manhattan office earlier that day, as soon as she'd found out—thanks to her father presenting it to her as a fait accompli over the phone. *'See, my darling? I've done it all for you! Now all you have to do is meet some nice young man!'* Lia had been ready to demand that all her details be removed...only to be informed that someone had already signalled his interest in dating her.

And Elizabeth Young had surprised Lia. She'd been expecting... Actually, she hadn't been sure what she'd been expecting of a billionaire matchmaker, but it hadn't been a beautiful young woman of around her own age, whose style reflected Lia's preferred classic relaxed elegance. Elizabeth Young had also personified professional discretion, which Lia had responded to in spite of herself.

And somehow, while acknowledging Lia's reluctance to accept the date, Elizabeth had somehow skilfully managed to persuade her to give this one date a chance. And then she'd shown Lia a picture of the man in question.

It had taken Lia a few long seconds to look past the piercing blue eyes and the boldly handsome and very masculine features. With his thick dark hair, he oozed sexy confidence and virility. Exactly the kind of man that Lia instinctively shied away from—because a personality like that brought up all her most secret vulnerabilities. And a reminder of another too confident personality who'd had no time for Lia's innate shyness—her mother, who had walked out on Lia and her father when Lia was just ten years old.

And yet she'd felt a disconcerting flutter of very feminine awareness at the man's sheer masculinity. It was most unwelcome. She wasn't interested in dating. She'd tried to please her father before—even going so far as to consider marriage, becoming engaged—but that had ended in abject humiliation when she'd surprised her fiancé in his office one day and found him with his face buried between his secretary's spread legs as she'd lain back across his desk, moaning loudly, her hands locked in his hair.

'You're frigid, Lia,' he'd hurled at her afterwards. *'I can't marry a woman who doesn't like sex!'*

That experience had only reinforced her insecurities, and she'd vowed since then to focus on her career and prove to her father that she could stand on her own two feet. Unfortunately his habitual ill health meant that she'd spent more time shoring up the family business than focusing on her own ambitions…

Elizabeth Young had brought Lia back to the present with a bump, though, when she'd revealed who the mysterious man was and recognition of his name had made Lia's gaze narrow on the woman on the opposite side of the desk. *'Benjamin Carter?* As in Carter Construction?'

Elizabeth Young had nodded. 'Yes, he said he knew of you, actually, even though he's never met you. He had some business with your father a while ago?'

Every protective hackle inside Lia had risen. It had been a couple of years ago when Benjamin Carter had come to the UK and tried to take over Ford Construction. Her family business. Her father had rebuffed Carter and his very generous offer, but his health, which had always been weak, and particularly weakened at that time, thanks to a nasty bout of pneumonia, had worsened.

If she'd met Benjamin Carter then she would have told him where to go and saved her father that relapse. Louis Ford was so proud, though, that he would have died before he'd let anyone see how frail he really was. Especially someone like the American construction mogul whom her father had described as 'formidable'.

And now Benjamin Carter wanted to meet her for a date? If this was mere coincidence then she was the Sugar Plum Fairy.

Lia stopped at a pedestrian crossing and forced herself to regulate her breath. She knew she could have just called the date off—instructed Elizabeth Young to inform Benjamin Carter that she wasn't available for any dates while she was in New York as she didn't live there—but she'd felt the compelling urge to inform the man emphatically and in person that there would be no route for him to get to her father. And certainly not through *her*.

On the other side of the street the majestic *beaux arts* Algonquin Hotel soared into the sky. They were due to meet in the darkly seductive Algonquin bar. And now all she could seem to think of was his boldly handsome features and those blue eyes. She found herself feeling slightly breathless, wondering how tall he would be. How big.

The pedestrian lights said *Walk* and Lia stepped into the road, assuring herself fiercely that Benjamin Carter would undoubtedly prove to be a disappointment in the flesh, as so many public figures did. *Not*, she hurriedly assured herself, that she was going to be hanging around long enough to check him out. No, she was going to waste no time informing him that—

Smack!

Lia's thoughts were scattered to pieces as she ran into a brick wall just outside the hotel. Gasping for air, she looked up to find that this particular brick wall was actually a very tall human. And very male. And very broad. With piercing blue eyes.

So not a wall at all. Dimly she registered that Benjamin Carter wasn't a disappointment in the flesh. Far from it. He was...*more*. He smiled, and she noticed the sculpted sensuality of his lips.

'I'm sorry, I hadn't planned on a collision as our introduction. I saw you crossing the street and recognised you from your photo, so I thought I'd wait for you. Are you okay?'

His voice was rich and deep enough to impact on her on a physical level. Lia felt a bit stupid, and put it down to the momentary shock and lack of breath. She nodded and managed to get out, 'Fine...just fine.'

She'd been so preoccupied with meeting him that she'd walked right into him. She realised then that her hands were wrapped around his arms to steady herself, obviously having landed there instinctively. She could feel hard biceps, even through the material of his overcoat, and she snatched her hands back as if they were burning.

He looked at her for a long moment and then stood back, indicating with a hand. 'Please—ladies first.'

Irritated that the wind had been knocked out of her—literally—Lia had no choice but to proceed to the front door, where a doorman was waiting, holding the door open, tipping his hat to her as she entered.

She heard him say to the man behind her, 'Welcome back, Mr Carter.'

'Thank you, Tom, always a pleasure.'

Lia felt like scowling at his smooth delivery, even though she had to acknowledge that her first cataclysmic encounter with the man didn't make her think of smooth at all. It had brought to mind lots of things—none of which were smooth. *Big, powerful, strong.* Immovable. That was what came to mind.

He was behind her now and she could smell his scent—as masculine as he was, and evocative more than overpowering.

The *maître d'* came forward to greet them at the entrance to the dark and lushly decorated bar, clicking his fingers for a staff member to come and divest them of their coats. Lia wanted to protest that she wasn't staying long, but before she could speak their coats had expertly been taken and she was being led further into the seductive space, to an intimate table for two at the back.

Giving in to the inevitability of at least explaining herself to this man, she slid into the velvet banquette seat at the wall and watched as Benjamin Carter folded his tall frame into a seat opposite her. She sucked in as much oxygen as she could, desperately hoping that her sense of equilibrium would return after the shock of that impact.

Now his coat was gone she saw that he wore a three-piece suit. Dark grey tie. She also recognised with a disturbing flash of heat, that in spite of his very suave exterior there was an unmistakable edge of something dangerous and uncivilised about the man. It was in the way his muscles pushed against the fabric of his jacket. As if he was more warrior than urbane businessman.

That realisation sent a shard of panic to her gut, and with a rush Lia started to speak. 'Look, Mr Carter—'

The words dried up when he held out his hand and smiled, drawing her gaze helplessly to his mouth. A full lower lip and a slightly thinner upper lip—diminishing any prettiness and giving him that sensual edge that made her aware of him in a way that no man had ever made her feel before. Certainly not her ex-fiancé.

'Forgive me. I never introduced myself properly, I'm Benjamin Carter.'

A lifetime of manners being drummed into her by her father and strict boarding schools couldn't let her ignore his hand. She reached out, intending it to be a sterile and quick transaction, but the first thing that registered when his hand encompassed hers was a surprising roughness, which only reinforced her impression of him being less civilised than he looked.

She felt a pulse throb between her legs…her intimate flesh reacting to his touch. It was so powerful that she pressed her thighs together, and her fingers tightened reflexively around his in reaction as she said faintly, 'I'm Julianna—Julianna Ford.'

As slim, feminine fingers tightened around his all Ben could think about was how it would feel when other, more intimate muscles would tighten around a more sensitive part of his anatomy. He'd never had such an immediately carnal response to a woman, but the feel of her slimly curvaceous body colliding with his outside the hotel had had an impact he couldn't ignore.

He'd seen her from across the street, an intent look on her face, a small frown between her eyes. And then, as her long legs had closed the distance between them, he'd been too mesmerised by her graceful movements to budge an inch.

And then she'd cannoned straight into him.

The lush imprint of her soft breasts against his chest was still vivid. As soon as their bodies had collided lust had hit him like an injection of adrenalin to his heart. And it hadn't been one-sided; he'd seen the effect on her too. Those widening shocked eyes. Her cheeks flooding with colour. Her hands tightening around his arms. She was tall enough for him to have just dipped his head down slightly to claim that provocative mouth, if he'd so wished.

And now he was drowning in dark blue eyes, glossy dark brown hair, pale ivory skin and that mouth, so sweetly curved it was all he could do not to sweep the table to one side and devour her right here.

She was stunning. Exquisite.

And she was pulling her hand back from his now with a little tug. He let her go, reluctantly.

A waiter came to take their drinks order. Julianna appeared flustered for a moment, and then quickly ordered a bourbon on the rocks. Ben ordered a soda water.

When they were alone again Ben dragged his

mind out of the carnal gutter and said, 'Thank you for agreeing to meet with me.'

She looked at him and his blood surged south and his flesh hardened. Ben cursed the rush of rogue hormones. It wasn't even as if she was wearing anything overtly provocative. A pale silk shirt that was buttoned to her throat and a dark pencil skirt. Discreet make-up and jewellery. High heels. Classic. Elegant. But as far as his libido was concerned she might as well be naked.

'Look—' she said, but was cut off when the waiter returned with their drinks, setting them down.

Ben noticed that she took a swift sip of the amber liquid before putting the glass down again.

She appeared edgy all of a sudden, and he made allowances for the fact that she was nervous, saying, 'I believe you're only here for a week? You're based in London?'

She swallowed and his eyes followed the movement. Even that small movement was graceful. Her refined elegance was impacting upon him somewhere deep. And it surprised him. He'd long ago rejected the cool upper-class beauties who thronged around him—drawn by the hard shell he knew he wore, hewn over years of hard graft as he'd remoulded himself into something much more durable. He knew they were attracted to the rough edges he'd acquired. They didn't want to know he'd once been one of them. They only wanted the thrill of thinking they were with someone vaguely *dangerous*. Rough. Someone whose industry was gritty. Base.

He took pleasure in rejecting them because he rejected that world—and yet here he was, sitting mere inches away from a woman who could put all those other society bitches in the shade with a mere arching of her elegant brow. And his blood was pumping so hard and so hot he could hardly think straight.

She looked at him and dark tendrils of hair trailed over her shoulders like silk. 'I...yes, I'm based in London. So, to be perfectly honest, I think this date is pretty redundant.'

It took a second for her cut-glass English accent to sink in—and her words. And then they did... along with the very cool expression on her face.

Ben blinked. 'So why agree to a date if it's redundant?'

Her gaze narrowed and she took a deep breath,

and despite the sudden chill in the air Ben's gaze helplessly dropped down to take in the press of those luscious breasts against the thin silk of her blouse.

'Because I wanted to meet you face to face and tell you that I know you met my father before, when you tried to take him over.'

Ben's gaze snapped back to her dark blue one. The heat in his blood simmered, not diminishing under the positively frosty vibes she was sending his way now. He hid his surprise that she'd registered the connection and shrugged nonchalantly. 'It's a small world.'

She sounded bitter. 'Evidently *too* small.' She took another sip of her drink, her fingers pale around the heavy glass.

Ben tensed. 'What exactly are you saying?'

Now she looked almost angry, with two spots of colour coming into her pale cheeks. 'What I'm saying, Mr Carter—' she put heavy emphasis on his name, as if he might still be under any illusion that things weren't deteriorating rapidly '—is that, based on your previous history with my father, you can't seriously expect me to believe that this date is pure coincidence?'

Ben thought of how mesmerised he'd been by that photo of her and felt exposed. Her cynicism shouldn't have surprised him, but somehow it did. He was on high alert now. Carefully, he said, 'I can't say that it's pure coincidence, no. I am aware of who you are—who your father is.'

She smiled, but it was hard. 'And so you saw an opportunity and grabbed it?'

Ben forced a smile too, in some kind of an effort to try and relieve the tension. 'Evidently you joined the Leviathan agency because you're interested in dating, I would have thought the fact that we have something in common is a good conversation-starter.'

Julianna's eyes glittered like dark sapphire jewels. 'Well,' she said coolly, 'I'm afraid I have no interest in starting any kind of conversation with you, Mr Carter. I came here merely to inform you of that, in case you'd be left in any doubt.'

With that, she downed the rest of her drink in one go and gathered up her bag, which was on the seat beside her.

She stood up and looked down at him. 'And as for my father—his position has not changed, so I suggest you seek your opportunities elsewhere.

Thank you for the drink, Mr Carter, I'll see myself out.'

Before Ben could fully process what was happening she was hitching her bag strap onto her shoulder and walking away from the table.

Ben finally stood up, his reflexes dulled, thanks to shock, and was just in time to see the anxious-looking *maître d'* helping her with her overcoat. Then she was walking out of the bar without a backward glance.

Ben looked at his watch incredulously. The date had lasted less than fifteen minutes.

He sat down again, her haughty accent reverberating in his head. *'I suggest you seek your opportunities elsewhere.'* If it wasn't so disturbing it would be funny, but the fact was that her father had been the furthest thing from his mind until she'd brought him up.

Julianna Ford, with her glacial dark blue eyes and her upper crust accent, had just pulled the rug out from under Ben's feet. And it was only now that he fully registered that last look she'd sent him—disdainful and dismissive. As if he wasn't fit to clean her shoes.

Ben signalled for the bill. It had been a long

time since anyone had looked at him like that and, even though he knew he should be writing Julianna Ford off as a spoilt rich bitch, his blood still ran hot. Hot with lingering lust, and hot with irritation that she'd lodged herself so neatly under his skin so quickly.

To say this date had morphed into something out of all expectations was an understatement.

Ben was grim as he walked out just seconds later. No one took him by surprise—certainly not a woman. And definitely not a woman he wanted.

Lia was still trembling from an overload of adrenalin as the yellow cab took her to her Central Park hotel. And her head felt light with the effects of the alcohol she'd drunk too quickly. It had provided the Dutch courage she'd needed, though, to say what she'd had to say to the most intimidating man she'd ever met.

Even now she could picture him lounging on the other side of the table, all sleek hard muscle and broad shoulders, sheathed in that suit that had done nothing to disguise his crackling virile energy. That sexy smile playing around his mouth.

She couldn't really believe she'd found the

wherewithal to stand and look down at him and deliver those parting words, or that she'd managed to walk out on rubbery legs. She'd been terrified they'd buckle underneath her before she could make it to the door.

She knew she could project an icy veneer of confidence when she needed to—it was a skill she'd honed after her mother had left, when Lia had overheard her saying cuttingly, 'Of course I'm not taking Lia with me. What can I do with a child who stutters and stammers and blushes every time someone looks at her?'

Even now, all these years later, Lia still felt the faint burn of shame mixed with humiliation. Her father's subsequent over-lavishing of attention and love upon her hadn't been able to remove the scar of that rejection, but Lia had never stuttered or stammered again from that day on. The blushing, though… She put a hand to her cheek and it felt hot. Seemingly she still had little control over that.

At least Benjamin Carter had stayed in his seat. The thought of having to say those words to him if he'd uncoiled to his full intimidating height made her throat go dry.

She might—hopefully—have convinced him

that he was less interesting than the fungus grow-ing under a rock, but her throbbing pulse told her that he was far from uninteresting to *her*. And, as successfully as she might have delivered her put-down, that was the real reason why she'd all but run from the hotel, stumbling to a stop outside in the cool autumn air, gulping for breath as if she'd just run a marathon, her heart still pounding.

Thankfully the doorman had hailed her a cab straight away and they were pulling up outside her hotel now. Lia paid and tried not to run into the hotel, feeling irrationally as if a large hand might land on her shoulder at any moment.

The fact that the whole encounter with the con-struction mogul had veered way out of her con-trol was not something she was going to dwell on. If she had had any tiny doubt that his request to meet her had been entirely innocent, it had been blasted apart by his poker-faced reaction when she'd told him she knew who he was and about his previous encounter with her father. He'd been unapologetic, that incisive gaze reading her reac-tion like a hawk.

So she was glad she'd gone there and met him. She'd done what she'd set out to do, leaving him in no doubt as to what she thought of any plan he might have to pursue her father.

Or her.

Lia ignored the weirdly hollow feeling in her belly and stepped into a blessedly empty lift. And as for her very unwelcome physical reaction…? The way she still felt jittery, as if her skin was too tight, too hot…? That was just the lingering after-effects of adrenalin.

A sense of futility rose up inside her, a hint of remembered humiliation. After all, she was frigid, wasn't she? She'd been told that in no uncertain language by the only man she'd ever slept with. And she had the memories of how her body had failed miserably to respond to his lovemaking to back it up. So he must be right.

The lift doors opened and Lia stepped out into the plushly carpeted corridor. As she let herself into her room she ruthlessly pushed down a very alien sense of something that felt awfully like… yearning.

Ben was back in his vast loft-style apartment a short time later. Sirens pierced the air from far below in the vibrant Meatpacking District, but he was oblivious. Pacing the floor. He'd taken off his jacket and tie, feeling constricted. His head was still full of Julianna Ford, and her cooler than cool aristocratic beauty. The memory of that haughty accent and the way she'd so icily dismissed him made him want to see her come undone, hear her voice hoarse from screaming his name.

Dammit. Since when had he grown such an active imagination?

But something else niggled at him—her hostility, and her immediate leaping to the conclusion that his motivation to date her had something to do with her father. Ben's conscience niggled, but he pushed it down—he hadn't tried to pretend to Julianna that he was unaware of who she was. He just hadn't mentioned it up front.

He thought again of how absent her father had been from view in the last few months and Julianna Ford's actions took on a much more intriguing light. She'd been…protective—and why would she feel the need to be protective unless her father was ill…weak?

Just then his phone vibrated in his pocket and he took it out, scowling when he saw the name *Elizabeth Young* on the screen.

When he answered she spoke straight away, sounding disapproving, 'I don't know what happened between you and Julianna Ford but she's instructed me that she doesn't want to meet with you again and to take her profile out of my portfolio.'

That made Ben feel simultaneously annoyed at the confirmation that she didn't want to see him again, and pleased that she obviously wasn't eager for a date with any other man. Also, it confirmed his suspicion that she had something to hide... some vulnerability. Because she perceived him to be a threat.

The unmistakable instinct to take up a challenge coursed through his blood. 'It's unfortunate that the date didn't go well, but I'll take it from here.'

Elizabeth Young was sharp. 'This is not how I conduct my business, Mr Carter. You can't pursue her if she's specifically requested not to see you again.'

Irritation prickled at this reiteration that she didn't want to see him again—*and* at the implication that anyone could tell him what to do. But Ben realised that he couldn't afford to alienate this woman. She was the key to all their futures.

Except right now he was determined to take his future into his own hands.

'You can rest assured, Miss Young. I won't pursue her again through your agency.'

There was silence for a moment, and then Elizabeth Young said, 'Thank you. If and when you're ready to date again we can set up another appointment. But, Mr Carter, I have to warn you that I won't tolerate anyone alienating my clientele.'

Once again Ben had to admit to a grudging sense of respect for the straight-talking matchmaker. Intimidated by powerful men she obviously was not. He said, 'Julianna Ford and I had a clash of personality—that's all. It happens from time to time. If I need you again I'll call you. Goodbye, Miss Young.'

Ben terminated the call, filled with resolve. A clash of personality it might have been, between him and the lustrous dark-haired British beauty, but electricity had sizzled between them, no matter how icy her demeanour. He knew Julianna Ford was here for a charity function, and New York could be a surprisingly small place when you moved in certain circles. If they happened to meet again it wouldn't be via Elizabeth Young, as he'd assured her.

Ben made a call on his phone, issuing curt instructions to his assistant on the other end. He told himself that the spiking of anticipation in his blood had more to do with the fact that Julianna Ford represented a chance to achieve his public and professional redemption and less to do with the fact that she'd intrigued the hell out of him with her frosty attitude—or the fact that he wanted her more than he'd ever wanted another woman.

CHAPTER TWO

THE FOLLOWING EVENING Lia surveyed herself critically in the full-length mirror of her hotel suite. The long evening dress was far more revealing than she liked, with its sleeveless plunging neckline and thigh-high slit, and also, if that wasn't enough, the vibrant blood-red colour.

But, as much as she squirmed to show so much flesh, she knew that it would be effective as a means of deflecting attention from the fact that her father was conspicuous by his absence at the charity auction he'd been due to attend in one of Manhattan's glitziest hotels.

She was also due to attend on her own behalf, because the charity—which helped crisis-stricken regions to begin rebuilding—was close to her heart.

She'd spoken to her father briefly and had been somewhat reassured. He was sounding a little perkier than he had in recent days. But this last stroke, albeit mild, had given them both a fright.

She'd told him that she'd gone on a date, and he'd been so delighted that she'd felt bad when she hadn't revealed who her date had been. The last thing he needed was to hear Benjamin Carter's name. Like her, he'd inevitably jump to the conclusion that he had ulterior motives—because the vultures were circling, just waiting for their chance to step in and make the most of Louis Ford's weakness.

Lia had confirmed it for herself when she'd done an internet search on Benjamin Carter late last night—unable to sleep because a leanly handsome face with piercing blue eyes had kept her awake.

She'd come across a recent paparazzi photo of Benjamin Carter together with three of the world's most notorious playboy tycoons and renowned business rivals. Xander Trakas, Dante Mancini and Sheikh Zayn Al-Ghamdi—all names that were indelibly linked to vast fortunes, beautiful women and an aversion to commitment.

The accompanying article had pointed out that they'd all suffered adverse press in recent months and speculation was rife as to why they were suddenly joining forces.

And that was when Lia knew she'd made a huge tactical error in showing Benjamin Carter such obvious antipathy. He was not becoming bosom buddies with his old enemies for no reason, nor asking her for a date for the good of his health—not when he could date any number of more beautiful and accessible women.

He was definitely up to something.

Curiously reluctant to leave her search there, though, she'd also learnt that he was a self-made legend who'd come from the most adverse of backgrounds, growing up in foster homes in Queens before working his way up through the construction hierarchy on sites all over New York. That had reminded her disturbingly of that air of something untamed about him in spite of his suave appearance.

Within just a decade he'd risen to the top of the industry—literally. His company was currently responsible for constructing what would become the tallest skyscraper in Manhattan.

He was ruthless and single-minded, and women only featured in his workaholic life as very momentary diversions—as brutally evidenced by a recent 'kiss and tell' Lia had found during the online search. Usually she abhorred gossip, but she'd found herself avidly reading about the way his ruthlessness extended beyond the bedroom once he was tired with seduction and conquest—which seemed to happen after only one or two dates at the most.

Yet that information hadn't stopped Lia having a very illicit and dangerously wistful daydream that when she'd bumped into him in the street perhaps Benjamin Carter might have been just a random gorgeous stranger. Because for the first time since the humiliating aftermath of her broken engagement, a year before, she realised that a man had managed to break through the high wall she'd built around herself.

Lia quickly shut down that evocative image. So, she'd reacted to him? All that proved was that she was as dismayingly susceptible to his charms as the next woman. In spite of her frigidity. Benjamin Carter's particular brand of virile masculinity was obviously potent enough to break through the thickest ice.

She glared balefully now at the extravagant vase

of flowers on the antique side table, set there by a conscientious staff member. The accompanying note lay torn up in the bin, but she didn't need to take it out to reread the arrogant slashing handwriting. She'd memorised it all too easily and annoyingly.

Till we meet again, Julianna. Ben.

The fact that he knew where she was staying caused little surprise. It wasn't as if she was using an alias, and a man like Benjamin Carter would have minions aplenty to do his dirty work.

She'd almost been tempted to call Elizabeth Young again, to tell her to reinforce the message that she had no interest in him, but she'd realised she was being ridiculous. As rough as Benjamin Carter's edges might be, she couldn't see him stooping so low as to actually *chase* a woman. And in a few days Lia would be gone—safely back on the other side of the Atlantic Ocean.

She turned her attention to her reflection again and took a deep breath, picking up an elaborately feathered black lace mask and fitting it to her face. She was relieved the charity auction had a masquerade theme, because she was feeling exposed enough as it was.

Firmly pushing disturbing memories back down where they belonged, along with thoughts of dark, handsome, annoying men, Lia gathered her things and left her suite.

Less than an hour later Lia had to stop herself from pulling the bodice of her dress up higher. She knew she was being silly, because there were women there in far more revealing dresses, but if one more man nearly tripped over his own tongue as he drooled at her chest she was going to scream.

Just then the three men who had been making more eye contact with her chest than her face seemed to melt back into the throng, and she sucked in a deep sigh of relief.

She turned away to look for a waiter and get a drink and found herself being jostled from behind. She was pitching forward helplessly into thin air when two hands caught her and stopped her fall. She looked up, heart hammering, to see a man—a very tall man, with broad shoulders. He was dressed in a white tuxedo jacket, white shirt and black bow tie.

His face, like most of the crowd's, was obscured by a mask. Except his was more ornate and covered his whole face. She could see thick dark hair… For a heart-stopping moment Lia almost suspected— But then she told herself she was being ridiculous if she was letting Benjamin Carter get to her so much that she suspected this man could be him, when it was far more likely to be a stranger.

The man spoke, his voice slightly distorted under the mask. 'Are you all right?'

Something inside Lia relaxed when she realised she didn't immediately recognise the voice. His hands felt hot on the bare skin of her upper arms and she realised he was still holding on to her. Feeling flustered, she took a step back. 'I'm fine, thank you… Sorry. I was just looking for a waiter to get a drink.'

'Let me.'

As if by magic a waiter appeared by his side and the man handed her a glass of Champagne. She noticed that he didn't take a drink. She sipped at the cool sparkling wine and felt some equilibrium return. Lia assured herself that if this *was* Benjamin Carter alarm bells would be ringing loudly.

She pushed all thoughts of that man aside and observed, 'You're not drinking?'

He shook his head. 'I like to keep my wits about me—and my mask isn't exactly conducive to drinking. I'd have to reveal my identity, which would defeat the object of the evening.'

His voice was cool, sardonic. And deep.

Something skated over Lia's skin. Excitement. She couldn't see his eyes, they were obscured, so she didn't know what colour they were. The realisation that she didn't even know where his eyes rested on her, or if he liked what he saw, made her skin heat with awareness. Before, she'd felt exposed, violated. Now she felt...aware of herself in a way that was very unlike her.

She almost had to suppress a slightly hysterical urge to giggle—maybe there was something in the water here in New York that was having an adverse effect on her?

'You could have chosen a less restrictive mask,' she pointed out to the stranger.

'I could have,' he agreed, leaving the words *But I didn't* hanging silently between them.

Bizarrely, she got the distinct impression that this stranger would bend for no one. A crazy thought to have about someone she'd only met for mere seconds. Someone whose face she couldn't even see. And crazy that it should send another shiver of excitement down her spine.

A hum of electricity infused her blood. Yesterday evening, when Benjamin Carter had precipitated similar sensations, she'd escaped as fast as she could. And now she was feeling all those things again. It was almost a relief—proof that his effect on her wasn't exclusive.

The crowd seemed to be pressing in around them, pushing them closer together. Heat prickled over Lia's skin in earnest now. A little panicked by her strong reactions, she said, 'It's getting claustrophobic in here, don't you think?'

'Would you like to get some air?'

Lia nodded, heart hammering. He expertly divested her of her half-empty glass and put a hand under her elbow. She found herself trying to assess if his palms were smooth or callused, but the crowd was jostling them too much. Then he was opening the French doors and leading her outside. It was late autumn, not quite yet winter, and the air was fresh. She moved away from him and gulped in deep breaths, her head feeling light. She put it down to the sparkling wine and the sudden rush of oxygen.

She went and put her hands on the stone wall, aware of the man coming to stand beside her, but keeping a distance that she appreciated. The lights of Manhattan sparkled around them, and Central Park was a dark shadow in the distance. There was silence between them for a moment, but it wasn't awkward. This unexpected encounter was taking on an unreal quality.

'I could never get tired of this view even if I lived here,' Lia said.

The man turned towards her. 'Where *do* you live?'

She glanced at him, finding the mask disconcerting but also a little…thrilling. Not knowing who she was speaking to was freeing, in some way. As if the normal social niceties could be ignored. The sheer breadth of his chest under his shirt made her hands itch. She felt very feminine next to his tall, broad body.

'I live just outside London, in Richmond.'

The man made an appreciative sound.

Lia smiled. 'You know it?'

She heard an answering smile in his voice. 'It's a nice place. Expensive.'

Lia commented dryly, 'The tickets for this event start at a cool six thousand dollars, so I'm guessing that you're no stranger to the more salubrious end of the property scale.'

Now he shrugged lightly. 'I can't deny that.'

Lia thought she saw the glitter of light eyes behind the mask and her heart beat a little faster. This felt risky...dangerous. But still thrilling.

She had never felt comfortable flirting, not having had her mother to guide her. She'd been so young when her mother had left them, and the all-girls weekly boarding school she'd attended hadn't done much to help her grow more comfortable around boys and men.

But at least by the time she'd left school the acute shyness that had blighted her earlier years had been largely a thing of the past. Although even now that awkward stuttering girl still lurked deep within Lia, reminding her of the fact that a lot of what she projected was an elaborate act.

It was an act so effective that her ex-fiancé had been incredulous to discover that she was a virgin when they'd had sex for the first time, which had only added to the mortification she'd felt when the experience had proved to be painful and generally underwhelming.

But now she felt confident, and a little reckless. 'So, is your role tonight to be as enigmatic and unrecognisable as possible?'

'Is it working?'

His tone was light, but Lia could sense an edge. It added to the air of illicit danger and excitement.

'Well, you've got the unrecognisable part down to a T.'

'Ouch,' he said softly. 'Clearly I have to work on being an enigma.'

Once again Lia had the distinct impression that being enigmatic came all too easily to this stranger. And he knew it. Even without seeing his face she could sense his sheer command and charisma. He was *somebody*.

She felt even more reckless as she said, 'Are we going to exchange names?'

'Do you want to?'

Lia nodded, and then shivered lightly. It was as if she could *feel* his gaze on her now, even though she couldn't see his eyes. It was like a caress across her skin.

Obviously misreading her shiver, he took off his jacket and settled it around her shoulders before she could protest. The heat from his body felt absurdly intimate, and she was acutely aware of his fingers brushing the bare skin of her shoulders.

Was it her imagination, or had they lingered a moment? 'Thank you.' Her voice was husky.

He was closer now—close enough that she could see his stubbled jaw under the mask. It looked strong, defined. His scent was masculine, woody and musky.

To her surprise she felt her lower body clench in reaction, and a rush of damp heat between her legs. That very physical reaction sent a dose of reality rushing back. This wasn't her. This wasn't a usual state for her to be in... For a second she wondered what had changed inside her. How could she be reacting so wantonly to two men in the space of two nights?

The stranger cut into her thoughts with his deep voice. 'Are you sure you want to exchange names?'

Lia wasn't so sure now. That slap of reality had reminded her that she was out of her depth here. But she wasn't ready to burst this sensual bubble yet. She was pretending to be something she wasn't—confident. Experienced.

Feeling absurdly regretful, she said, 'I'm not sure if I do…but we can't hide for ever…'

She heard the smile in his voice again. 'It's tempting, though, isn't it?'

She nodded, feeling something melting inside her at the sense of kinship she felt. She desperately wanted to keep pretending to be someone else for another small moment, and helplessly she found her feet moving closer.

He seemed to reach for her at the same time, and his hands cupped her jaw, thumbs caressing her cheeks. 'You're exquisite—do you know that?'

Lia shook her head, embarrassed. She knew without false modesty that she was pleasant enough to look at, but she'd never felt truly beautiful. She looked at women sometimes and saw that they owned their innate sensuality in such a way that she envied them. And it had nothing to do with being the perfect size or having a pretty face.

But right now…even though half her face was obscured by a mask…she felt an inkling of it. For the first time. Her mouth tingled and she imagined his gaze on her there. Her lips parted and his hands tightened on her face. An urgency seemed to infuse the air around them…the atmosphere grew thick and heavy.

Excitement rushed through her. Lia reached up one hand, to touch his mask. Her heart thumping so hard she wondered if he could hear it, she started pushing it up, desperately wanting to see him, wanting his mouth to touch hers.

She caught a glimpse of his lower lip and then one hand wrapped around her wrist, stopping her. His voice sounded rough. 'You might not like what you see.'

Lia shook her head. She *knew*, just knew that she needed to see who he was more than she needed to draw breath. She pulled her hand free and was about to tip his mask up again when a voice broke through the thick tension.

'*Lia!* There you are. I've been looking everywhere for you! I'm having a total crisis—you have to help me.'

The mood snapped instantly. The man stepped back and Lia's hand dropped to her side. Her heart was racing as if they had just kissed, and she realised she was trembling.

She tore her eyes away from that impassive mask that hid so much and she wanted to shout her frustration. She could see now that the person interrupting them was the charity auction event manager—an English ex-pat called Sarah, who had become a friend of sorts. They met whenever Lia came to New York.

'What's wrong, Sarah?' Lia was relieved that her voice sounded calmer than she felt.

The attractive blonde woman looked panicked. 'Stacy Somers, the supermodel, was supposed to be here for the charity auction, which is due to start in ten minutes. The deal was that she'd auction a kiss, and now we're stuck.'

Lia's eyes widened at her friend's expressive look, and she spluttered, 'But...but you can't mean for *me* to fill in?' All her old insecurities flooded back. 'I'm hardly supermodel-replacement material—and hardly anyone here even knows me!'

Her friend's eyes were wild and panicked. 'Please, Lia. You look amazing tonight, and no one will care who you are. It's for charity, and it's a fun item, and it's in the auction brochure and my boss is going crazy at the thought of the schedule getting messed up...'

Lia felt cornered. Just the thought of everyone staring at her made her skin break out in a cold sweat.

And then a deep voice from beside her said, '*I'd pay for a kiss from you.*'

She looked up at the man—she'd almost forgotten he was there in her moment of panic. And now she felt hot all over. At the thought of his eyes on her. At the thought of him claiming her in front of everyone. *Lord*. New York was warping her brain completely.

'I'm sorry, but who are you?'

The question came from Sarah, and Lia's attention snapped to her suddenly very curious-looking friend. The thought of him revealing who he was here and now threatened to burst the intimate bubble that had cocooned them.

Lia made a split-second decision and said, 'I'll do it.'

Her friend looked at her and her relief was palpable. Lia shrugged off the jacket and handed it back to the stranger. Their hands touched and she felt a zing of electricity. She felt jittery, as she had last night. Had she just sent him a challenge? Would he bid for a kiss and reveal himself?

Before she could think about it any further Sarah was taking her by the arm and all but hauling her back into the thronged room, gabbling about what she needed Lia to do. Lia barely heard a word.

She glanced back once before she was sucked into the crowd, but when she did the patio was empty and she wondered for a crazy, panicky moment if she'd just dreamed up the whole encounter with the enigmatic stranger. And, if she'd ever see him again.

'Now, who is going to start the bidding for a kiss with our lovely English rose, Julianna Ford?' said the smooth-voiced auctioneer behind the tall lectern.

Benjamin stood at the side of the room with his arms folded and his hands tucked under his arms. Because he was afraid he might reach out and throttle anyone who dared to attempt to kiss the woman standing on the dais, situated in the centre of the vast room.

She looked far too enticing with her hair pulled back, exposing her long neck, but also strangely vulnerable. He would have thought that someone from her background and particular social scene would be accustomed to showing off in such a manner. She'd certainly shown an authoritative side when they'd met the previous evening.

And yet he recalled her wide-eyed look of shock just after they'd collided. The way colour had washed into her cheeks. Most women he knew would have made the most of such an encounter, but she'd appeared slightly awkward. Unsettled.

She wore an elaborate black lace mask over the top half of her face and it only enhanced her beauty, making her look mysterious. But even the mask couldn't hide the brilliant blue of her eyes. Or that enticing mouth.

He could sense other men's interest and a surge of something completely alien rushed up inside him. It took him a moment to recognise that it was possessiveness, because he'd never felt it before for a woman.

Mine. The word thrummed through Ben's blood, just as a voice near the front shouted out, 'Five thousand dollars!'

Something went tight inside Ben as the bidding started to escalate... *Ten thousand, fifteen... twenty...* There were gasps now, people were looking around.

And then a booming voice called out, 'Fifty thousand dollars!'

Ben knew who it was immediately. An old foe of his—someone who had tried to stamp out Ben's company before it had even got started. He saw the man pushing through the crowd now, small and squat, eyes bulging, perspiration beading on his brow.

He also saw, even from where he was, how Julianna's eyes widened behind the mask as she took him in.

The auctioneer held up his gavel and asked if anyone wanted to contest this latest bid. No one moved. The thought of that man getting anywhere near Julianna made Ben feel a level of violence he hadn't experienced in a long time.

The auctioneer brought the gavel down once, twice… And just before he could bring it down again Ben spoke authoritatively into the silence. 'One million dollars.'

Everyone gasped and turned to look at him. He walked forward, the crowd parting to let him through.

When he was near the dais he stopped and said,

'But I want more than a kiss. For a million dollars I want a weekend with Julianna Ford.'

It was him. She hadn't imagined him. She'd looked for him in the crowd as people had bid for the kiss, squirming with embarrassment but trying not to let it show. All the confidence and bravado she'd felt out on the terrace had faded under the glare of lights and hundreds of people.

But he was here. Still in the mask, like so many others. *Who was he?*

As if reading her thoughts, he said, 'If you agree to the bid I'll reveal myself.'

Her heart palpitated. She'd wanted this, hadn't she? She'd never felt so exposed in her life, and yet so tempted to throw caution to the wind and act completely out of character. Apart from anything else, the promise of a million dollars as a donation to her favourite charity was mind-boggling.

There was a discreet cough from nearby and the auctioneer said, 'Miss Ford? Do you accept this bid? It's a little unorthodox…'

Feeling as if she was taking a giant leap off a cliff and into the unknown, she nodded her head jerkily before she could lose her nerve. She was barely aware of the auctioneer wrapping up the bidding—because who on earth would bid more than a million dollars? It was crazy, outrageous.

Romantic, said a small voice that she quickly shut down. Since when had she been interested in *romantic*? Certainly not after seeing the devastating effects of her mother leaving her father...

And now the auctioneer was saying, 'I think we'd all like to know who our mysterious benefactor is—not least Miss Ford, who has to spend a weekend with you.'

Slightly nervous laughter rippled through the crowd as the man reached up to pull his mask off. Just before he did, Lia caught a flash of light blue eyes and a shiver of foreboding skated down her spine.

No. It wouldn't be. It couldn't be.

But the mask came off and there seemed to be a collective sigh of female appreciation as Benjamin Carter was revealed in all his dark masculine beauty. All his dark, masculine, *smug* beauty.

Lia felt as if she'd been punched in the belly. The fact that it had been *him* all along was something she couldn't quite assimilate yet. Or didn't want to. It was too huge. And now she was being ushered off the dais so that they could get to the next item on the auction list.

The charity's CEO approached Lia with suspiciously bright eyes, pumping her hand, telling her she had no idea what this would mean for them, and all Lia could think was, *I'm going to kill him.*

However embarrassed she'd been, standing up in front of that crowd, she writhed with mortification inside to think of the ridiculous flight of fancy she'd taken for a moment, that some enigmatic stranger wanted her enough to bid a million dollars for her company.

Just then a large, warm, *callused* hand curled around her elbow and she went rigid as sensation shot through her—and the galling confirmation that it was *his* touch alone that seemed to affect her, and not some general awakening of latent desires.

She tried to tug her arm free but his grip tightened and another shiver went through her—not entirely unpleasant. She refused to look at him, though, even as the CEO of the charity was gushing all over him.

He said smoothly, 'I was inspired by Miss Ford's dedication—offering herself up for the good of the charity—and as you know this cause is close to my heart.'

Lia just bet it was. *Not*. She wanted nothing more than to round on Benjamin Carter and tell him exactly what she thought of his outrageous stunt, but she couldn't. Not after such a public display of largesse.

Finally he was moving away from the CEO and taking Lia with him, walking out of the function room. People looked and whispered. Lia caught more than a few envious glances and felt like saying, *You're welcome to him!* But she gritted her jaw and kept moving.

As soon as they were outside the room, Benjamin Carter walked her over to a secluded corner of the lobby, where tall plants shielded them from general view. Lia finally managed to pull free and turned on him, steeling herself not to react to his sheer magnetism.

For a second she couldn't get a word out, she was so incensed. She plucked at the ribbons of her mask behind her head and pulled it off. She felt very bare without its protection, but ignored it.

Benjamin Carter's gaze had lowered to where her chest was heaving with indignation and shock.

She folded her arms pointedly. 'What the *hell* do you think you're doing?'

He raised his gaze and put his hands in his pockets, supremely at ease. He drawled, 'Apart from displaying immense generosity, I would have thought the rest was fairly obvious.'

'*That*,' Lia spat out, 'was the most ostentatious, crass demonstration of wealth I've ever seen in my life.'

Something tightened in his expression, but Julianna didn't feel regret.

'You didn't look especially enthralled at the thought of kissing Saul Goldstein.'

She fought not to shudder at the image in her head of the other man's fleshy mouth. She tipped up her chin. 'I would choose to be kissed by him any day of the week rather than spend a minute in your company.'

He made a mocking sound. 'Such strong feelings, Lia…'

She cursed her out-of-control emotions, feeling heat climb into her cheeks at the thought that she was behaving far beneath her usual levels of decorum. Even so, she said, 'Only friends and family call me Lia—and you're neither.'

He put a hand to his chest. 'I'm wounded...'

Lia all but snorted. She couldn't imagine *anything* wounding this man. He was like a force of nature. Immune to any kind of threat. And certainly immune to her sustained animosity, which she was very afraid stemmed from a place that had nothing to do with the threat to her father's business and everything to do with a far more personal threat.

'You didn't have to accept the bid,' he pointed out. Annoyingly.

Lia unfolded her arms to put her hands on her hips. 'You didn't reveal your identity until *after* I'd accepted the bid. How could I then turn down a million dollars for the charity?' She shook her head, desperate not to let him guess for a second what deeper desires had led her to accept the bid. 'You painted me into a corner, Mr Carter. I had no choice.'

His eyes gleamed bright blue against the olive tones of his skin. 'We always have a choice, *Lia*.'

His insistence on goading her seemed to get lost for a second in the way he said her name, making her think of how intimate it had felt to talk to him out on that terrace. She decided that his calling her Lia was a lesser battle and not to be fought right now.

She started to pace, feeling edgy. So much for believing earlier that her antipathy would have somehow magically signalled to her who she was dealing with. She stopped and looked at him accusingly. 'You completely tricked me from the moment you came up to me, hiding behind your mask. Why didn't you tell me who you were?'

'Why didn't *you*?' he riposted.

Lia made a sound of frustration and her hands became fists at her sides. 'You had an unfair advantage with your mask. Obviously you don't experience many women walking out on dates with you, but if this is just because your pride is dented then—'

'Don't be ridiculous.'

The steel underlying his deep voice stopped Lia.

'You really think I'd be so petty that I'd pay an extortionate amount of money just to buy a weekend with a woman who walked out on a date?'

The man in front of her bristled with lots of things…none of which was pettiness. Lia was suddenly aware that she wasn't sure if she wanted to know exactly why Carter *had* paid all that money for her.

'There's not going to *be* a weekend,' she said tightly. 'It's ridiculous to think that I would go off with a complete stranger. Everyone will appreciate that it was just a stunt.'

He shook his head and came closer to Lia. She fought to stand her ground and not back away. He was so close now that the disparity in their sizes was apparent again. It brought back the memory of standing on the patio and looking up…aching to feel his mouth on hers…reaching up to take his mask off and having his hand close around her wrist… It was as if she'd blocked it out at the time, but she realised now that she *had* felt the rough skin of his palms on her skin. But she'd ignored it.

The fact that less than an hour ago she'd been reaching up to kiss him made her feel exposed all over again. She couldn't even contemplate the suspicion that on some level she'd known who he was all along.

Lia was aware that her reactions to this man were completely out of her control, but she couldn't seem to rein herself in. This close to him, she couldn't focus. All she could feel was the threat to her equilibrium and the desire to get away from him. Far away.

'Look,' she said, purposely making her voice as chilly as possible, 'I don't know how things work here in America, but in England we don't really go in for such crass displays of wealth. I appreciate that you've undertaken to donate a lot of money to the charity, but there is simply no way that I am going to go *anywhere* with you—a million dollars or not.'

She folded her arms again and regarded Benjamin Carter as best she could from several inches less in height.

Benjamin Carter, damn him, just smiled.

'There's no need to be patronising, sweetheart.'

Heat washed up over her chest and neck. She'd never usually descend to such rudeness, but this man, under his guise as a stranger, had seen her react in a way that made her want to crawl under a rock and hide.

'And, yes' he said now, 'you *are* coming with me. Because if you don't I will tell the charity's CEO that contrary to your public acceptance of the bet, you're not actually willing to fulfil your end of the bargain and therefore I will be withdrawing my funds.'

All the heat left Lia's body as her blood rushed south. 'You wouldn't dare. Not when everyone knows how much you donated.'

He took his hands out of his pockets and folded his arms across his chest. 'Do you really want to test me?'

Right now he looked as immovable as a mountain. And Lia had serious doubts about what he would do if she *did* test him. Clearly a man like this, who could make such obscenely huge gestures, was beholden to no one and wouldn't hesitate to prove his point.

Feeling utterly cornered and trapped, Lia said, 'Why are you doing this…? If it's not for spite… then what?'

He looked at her for a long moment and she couldn't read his expression.

Then he said, 'It's very simple, Lia. I want you.'

CHAPTER THREE

THE AIR SIZZLED between them and Ben's very direct words seemed to hang between them like a dare. What was it about this woman that seemed to arouse the beast in him? That made him do crazy things like pretend to be a stranger? And make outrageous public bids?

Her eyes were huge, as if she was still absorbing what he'd said, and then she responded, with a frigid tone to her voice. 'You want me enough to pay one million dollars for the pleasure? I don't know who you're used to consorting with, or who you think I am, but I'm not some kind of high-class—'

'I know *exactly* who you are,' he said curtly, cutting her off, surprised at the rapid surge of anger her insinuation had provoked.

It had been a long time since he'd felt the need to justify himself to anyone—much less to someone who came from the same part of society that had turned its back on him and left him to fend for himself. In that respect England and America were one and the same.

Nevertheless, he couldn't stop himself saying stiffly, 'I've never paid for a woman in my life. I don't need to.'

Intriguingly, she blushed, and suddenly she didn't look so confident. 'What do you mean, you know exactly who I am?'

The nerve she'd struck, however inadvertently, made him say, 'You might not be royalty but you're a princess. Someone who has probably been denied nothing in her whole life. You don't like me because I turn you on, and you don't like being turned on by someone you consider beneath you.' He continued, 'Out on that terrace, before my identity was revealed, you had no prejudices holding you back because evidently you had judged that I was someone a little more...*refined*.'

The play of reactions across her face was mesmerising. Shock. Anger. Insult. And then fire. 'You played with me like a cat with a mouse. And, in light of your opinion, I fail to see why you'd want to subject yourself to spending a whole weekend with me.'

Lia went to move around him, to get away, but he stopped her with a hand on her arm. Her skin was silky smooth and warm, her arm slender under his hand. He felt crass then, and boorish. Not fit to touch someone as exquisite as her. But he held on and she swung around to face him, eyes flashing.

'Let me go, *damn you*. And for the record, you don't turn me on—not in the slightest.'

A challenge to disprove her rose hot and urgent through his body and Ben put both hands on her arms. But then, through the obvious anger she displayed, he caught a glimpse of something else in those stunning eyes…something almost like *hurt*. Hurt that he'd been accurate in his assessment of her and she wasn't used to hearing the bald truth? Or because he'd got it wrong?

He forced a modicum of civility back into his overheated brain. 'I didn't mean what I said as a personal attack. You're a product of your upbringing, that's all, and I was merely pointing out that I'm well aware that you're the furthest thing imaginable from a high-class hooker.'

That curious expression faded from her eyes, making Ben feel foolish for suspecting for a second that he'd hurt her because he'd got her wrong, and then she tensed under his hands, as if to leave again, and everything in him rejected it. The urge to disprove her assertion that she didn't want him was calling to the most primitive part of him.

'But I'm afraid I can't accept the lie.'

'What lie?' Now she looked wary.

'*This* lie.' And then he hauled her right into his body and covered her mouth with his.

Everything that had just passed between them was forgotten as the world seemed to combust into white heat. All Ben could feel was the press of that soft lush mouth and her body, moulding to his as if made for him alone.

All Lia could feel at first was steel, and then she realised it was the sheer hard-muscled strength of Benjamin Carter's body against hers, his hands tight on her arms. Her body was pressed so closely to his that her breasts were flattened against his chest, her nipples tingling from the contact.

And then, as if encouraged by the fact that she wasn't pulling away, his hold gentled minutely and his mouth became less of a searing brand and started to move on hers. Lia knew that she should be using this as an opportunity to pull free, stand back, demand to know what the hell he thought he was doing—especially after that heated exchange... But, treacherously, she didn't. Or couldn't.

One of his arms was sliding around her back now, pulling her in closer. And before she could stop herself she was responding to his kiss, her mouth softening and opening, and at the first touch of his tongue to hers she had no hope of remaining sane. Lia realised she was clutching at something to stay standing and that it was his arms, his biceps bulging under the material of his jacket, reminding her of the awesome power of his body.

There was something about this evidence of his sheer unadulterated masculinity that made her feel very feminine. It was seriously addictive. Yet the fact that she found his very masculine differences so attractive was unexpected and disorientating.

Certainly her ex-fiancé had never made her feel this...hot, or this desperate. This was wholly new and all too treacherously exhilarating.

Benjamin Carter's hand was cradling the back

of her head now, and his other hand was on her hip, fingers digging into her flesh. She could feel his erection against her and it didn't shock her—it made her want to move against him. She wanted to feel him notch it against her, between her legs where she felt slick and swollen. She felt a curious hollowness, a desire to be filled...

His kiss was rough and smooth all at once. And it was only when his mouth left hers and he started to press kisses along her jaw, when her head fell back in weak supplication, that she seemed to come to her senses. A voice screamed at her. *What the hell are you doing?*

She jerked away from him abruptly and took a shaky step back, staring at him, aghast. Her mouth felt swollen and she realised the top of her dress was dislodged, revealing the swell of her breast. She pulled it back up with a jerk. Her hair was half undone and she noticed the black mask she'd been wearing lying on the ground nearby. She was unravelling. And she'd just betrayed herself, spectacularly.

In a thready voice she said, 'I don't know what that was...'

'I do.'

Carter was grim, and Lia hated it that he looked as if he hadn't just fallen apart—not like her.

'That was me proving that I *do* turn you on—and unfortunately proving it to the rest of the world too.'

Lia went still. 'What do you mean?'

Carter glanced back at something she couldn't see and then looked at her again. 'I think we've been papped.'

She went cold. The thought of someone witnessing that intensely private moment when she'd been so vulnerable made her want to squirm. It was too much exposure in one night—especially on the heels of how deeply his words had cut when he'd told her exactly what he thought of her: *'You might not be royalty but you're a princess.'* She knew that she hadn't helped matters by reacting so defensively to him, but she was far from some pampered princess, and the fact that his opinion somehow mattered was even more infuriating.

She glared at him. 'This is all your fault. If you hadn't pursued me and made that ridiculous bid this wouldn't have happened.'

He had the gall to shrug one shoulder, and a devilishly sexy smile tipped his mouth up at one side. 'Sweetheart, I just proved there's enough electricity between us to power a small nation, so it was inevitable.'

Lia started to pace again, as much to convince herself that her legs were still working as anything else. Then she stopped and looked at him. 'I'm not your sweetheart, and I've had enough. I'm leaving.'

This time he didn't try to restrain her, he just said with deadly efficiency from behind her, 'I really wouldn't do that if I were you.'

Something in his voice made Lia stop. She looked longingly at the entrance to the hotel and felt her neck prickle under his gaze. With the utmost reluctance she turned around and said, as nonchalantly as she could, 'And why would that be?'

He folded his arms and said, 'You've agreed to the terms of a very public auction and I'm really not joking when I say that I'll renege on my bid if you don't fulfil your end of the agreement. You'll be followed and mercilessly tracked by the paparazzi.'

He took a step closer to Lia and she fought against his physical magnetism. The memory of his tongue, thrusting into her mouth with a kind of possessive intensity was still vivid, and she hated it that it was.

'And,' he continued, 'I know you're here till after the weekend, and that you have nothing else on your schedule—except presumably shopping. So you have no reason to refuse to take a trip with me.'

His sheer obduracy made Lia want to stamp her foot. As did his casual judgement of her—again. *Shopping!* Clearly he'd checked up on her—but only at the most superficial level—and the thought of the lengths to which he was prepared to go caught her in her solar plexus before she crushed it. No doubt he'd laugh his head off if she told him that she'd actually planned to go to a series of lectures at NYU on advances in sustainable temporary emergency structures.

This was all just the means to some nefarious end, chemistry or no chemistry. She could see that under his devastating charisma there was a merciless streak, and a sense of futility filled her. Look at what he'd done so far! She didn't doubt any more that if she walked away then he *would* take back his one million dollars.

Something about the fact that he thought he had her so neatly squared away in a little box was actually somewhat comforting; he wasn't anywhere close to seeing the real her. If she had to put up with his overbearing and cocky arrogance for a weekend for the sake of a greater good, then she could do it.

She just wouldn't be so susceptible again. And she certainly wouldn't be kissing him again.

Hitching up her chin, she said as icily as she could, 'It would appear that you leave me no choice in the matter. When do we leave and where are we going?'

Something that looked awfully like triumph flashed in Benjamin Carter's eyes as he strode towards her and took her arm in his hand again, propelling her forward and saying, 'There's no time like the present. We'll go to your hotel first, so you can pick up some essentials and your passport.'

Lia stopped in her tracks, forcing him to stop too, and he looked back at her, clearly impatient. Mindful of the people around them in the lobby, Lia hissed, *sotto voce*, 'Passport? Where on earth are you taking me?'

There was a definite glint of devilry in his eye as he said, 'Now, that would take all the fun out of it, don't you think? Don't worry, Lia, you'll be quite safe with me.'

She shivered minutely. She was afraid that she'd never been less safe—and it had nothing to do with physical safety…it was the sensual threat he posed and her own weakness to it. She was terrified of the way he made her feel so off balance. Out of control.

Fiercely, she said, 'Nothing is going to happen this weekend, Mr Carter. No matter what you believe. That kiss was a mistake.'

He smiled, and it was distinctly wolfish. 'I've never had to force a woman into my bed and I'm not about to start. Whatever happens will be completely mutual, I assure you.'

And then, before she knew what was happening, she was being handed her wrap and they were at the entrance of the hotel, where Carter opened the passenger door of a sleek dark grey sports car.

Holding herself rigid as she passed him, she got in with as much dignity as she could and in her head called him every name under the sun as he slammed her door shut and walked around the front of the car with lithe animal grace.

When he slid in beside her, bringing with him that tantalising musky scent, Lia held herself even more rigid. She could feel him glance at her and she stared straight ahead, vowing that with every fibre of her being she would resist this man and keep the vulnerable core of herself intact.

Whatever his game was, she wasn't interested in playing.

There had been nothing but a frosty silence interspersed with the barest of monosyllabic answers from the woman who was now curled up in a seat on the opposite side of Ben's private plane, looking out of the window, with her wrap pulled tightly around her, her hair down around her shoulders. Tousled dark silkiness...

Irritation and something more indefinable lay under Ben's skin at the thought that she wouldn't be here if he hadn't publicly paid a million dollars for the pleasure. But he pushed that aside. She was here now—that was all that mattered.

They'd taken off from a private airfield near Newark about an hour ago, after they'd gone to her hotel suite so that she could collect her passport and some essentials. She'd been about to go into the bathroom to change out of her dress when something perverse had made Ben say, 'We don't have time for that.'

She'd looked at him, blue eyes sending a flash of dark icy fire, and then, to give her her due, she'd merely stalked out of the suite, leaving her bags for him to pick up.

She was playing the role of princess to the hilt, and he had no one to blame but himself after he'd called her one. That enigmatic look in her eyes came back to him, the sense that she'd been hurt. His conscience pricked, even as he told himself that the women he knew from her kind of world were hardened.

But he had to admit that she was an intriguing mass of contradictions. Not least of which was the contradiction he'd met while they'd been wearing their masks. He had to acknowledge a little uncomfortably that he *had* had an advantage, having recognised her from the first moment. He'd intended to tell her who he was, but then she'd been so surprisingly sweet. And flirtatious. *Hot*. It had been a stark contrast to their first meeting—

confirming that he'd never really stood a chance, because she'd gone there only to warn him off.

But then, when she hadn't realised who he was, he'd been loath to ruin the mood by revealing his identity. Ben scowled now. It wasn't like him to give in to weak impulses. The whole object of this exercise was to seduce her, and ultimately—possibly—marry her.

Although right now the idea of this woman submitting to a life of domestic bliss with Ben seemed to be a stretch too far, even for his imagination. Surely this was the point when he decided she wasn't worth the trouble? There was any number of ex-lovers who'd made no attempt to hide their desire to become Mrs Carter...and yet Ben found he was curiously reluctant to let Lia go.

He wanted her. And the thought of taming her sharp tongue and making her acquiescent and pliant with desire was more arousing than anything he could remember.

He finally looked away from the disturbing provocation of the woman on the other side of the aisle and yanked at his bow tie, undoing it. He felt petty now, for not letting her change earlier. It wasn't exactly helping to douse his desire, knowing that just under the slimmest of coverings that tantalising body was—

'There were no paparazzi, were there?'

Ben jerked his head round to find those cool blue eyes narrowed on him, and saw that her arms were folded. Some of the tension inside him loosened and he turned towards her, seeing how her gaze involuntarily darted down and then back up.

She wanted him. And he would prove it to her.

Feeling only the tiniest prick of his conscience, Ben said, 'If you remember, I said I *thought* we'd been papped.'

Her eyes flashed. 'I can't believe I fell for it.'

Ben shrugged and took a sip of his coffee. 'You still wouldn't have had a choice in the end.'

That lush mouth tightened and Ben had to restrain himself from reaching across to touch it, make it soften. He thought of something then, and said, 'I like that you're called Lia. It's less…rigid.'

Those ivory cheeks flushed. 'Like I said, that's for friends and family.'

Ben smiled, enjoying her discomfiture more than he should. 'I think we're definitely more than friends now, *Lia*. I don't know what you're used to, but in my world friends don't kiss the way we did earlier. Lovers…now, that's a different matter.'

Lia darted a glance behind her, to where the discreet staff were, and then hissed across the aisle, 'We will never be lovers, Mr Carter.'

Ben ignored that and sat back, extending his legs, making himself comfortable even though the last thing he was feeling was relaxed. 'There's a bedroom at the back of the cabin. You should slip into something more comfortable and get some rest. We'll be in the air for another seven hours at least.'

'You're still insisting on not telling me where we're going?'

Ben glanced at her with mock innocence. 'And ruin the surprise?'

Her jaw clenched. 'I don't like surprises, Mr Carter.'

'Please, Lia,' he purred, enjoying himself immensely, 'call me Ben.'

After a long moment, when she looked as if she was seriously tempted to do him some physical violence, she undid her seat belt and stood up, saying, 'You're impossible. *This* is impossible.'

She took her bag from an overhead locker and

the wrap over her dress fell to the floor. Ben let his gaze roam freely over her curves, in particular her pert behind.

She whirled around and he looked up. She grabbed the wrap from him as he picked it up and held it out to her, and said tersely, 'I'm going to get some sleep. And I don't want to be disturbed.'

Ben smiled. 'Please, be my guest.'

Lia walked to the back of the plane, her red dress swirling about her body and those long slim legs. She went into the bedroom and the door was shut forcefully enough behind her to make Ben wince slightly. Then he heard the distinct *click* of the lock being turned.

His smile slipped from his face as he had to shift his body to accommodate his erection. He felt feral enough to be tempted to go and kick open the door and prove to Lia right now that they were more than *friends*. But he reminded himself that he was civilised.

After all, he had to acknowledge bitterly, for the first twelve years of his life Ben had been exceedingly civilised. Until everything had changed and the real world had been revealed, like in *The*

Wizard of Oz, when the curtain had been pulled back to expose the truth.

Just then Ben's phone vibrated and he welcomed the distraction. He took it out of his pocket to see a name flashing on the screen. He smiled mirthlessly and answered, 'Trakas. Are you missing me and our new friends already?'

'Hardly,' came the dry response. 'The internet is buzzing about you making some outrageous bid at a charity auction and absconding with a British society princess for the weekend. I thought we were trying to improve our reputations, not make them worse.'

Ben looked pointedly at the closed door of the bedroom and said through a tight jaw, 'Don't worry, it's all part of the plan. Elizabeth Young set us up on a date. Was there something in particular you wanted or did you just call to gossip?'

Xander Trakas was silent for a moment, and then he said, 'And…? How was she?'

Ben frowned. 'Who? The matchmaker?'

Trakas sounded impatient. 'Of course.'

Ben felt another pang of his conscience when he thought of what she'd think of his pursuing Lia in spite of her warning. 'She was fine. Why the hell do you care anyway?'

'No reason,' came the swift response, and then the other man said, 'Later, Carter,' and hung up.

Ben shook his head and put his phone down, glancing at the shut door again and scowling. He had no idea what was going on between Xander Trakas and the Leviathan Solutions director, but if it was anything close to what he was currently engaged in, then he wished the man luck. From what he'd seen of Elizabeth Young, and her quiet but steely self-possession, he'd need it.

'Let me show you around.'

Lia looked suspiciously at Benjamin Carter, who had no right to look so fresh and gorgeous after sleeping in his seat on the plane. He'd changed out of his tuxedo into dark trousers and a black short-sleeved polo shirt, and she was acutely aware of the bunching of his biceps where his arms were folded. He was even more powerful than she'd thought.

Stalling for time, to let her disorientated brain catch up with events, she said, 'Where exactly are we?'

They'd landed at Salvador International Airport in Bahia, Brazil, about an hour before, and to find out how far they'd come had blown her mind. Then Carter had collected an open-top Jeep and driven them out of the city and along the coast for about thirty minutes. Lia didn't like to admit that she'd been captivated by the Atlantic sea frothing against miles and miles of pristine beaches.

'We're at my private villa, north of Salvador.'

His blue gaze dropped momentarily down her body and Lia regretted not changing when she'd had the chance on the plane. But after pacing in the spacious bedroom for long minutes she'd given in to fatigue and had lain down on the bed, still in the dress. Then, when a peremptory knock on the door had woken her, and a too-familiar deep voice had told her they'd be landing soon, something petty in her had refused to make him feel more comfortable about what he'd done, so she'd emerged still wearing the dress.

But now she felt silly. And self-conscious. It made her say defiantly, 'What's to stop me from taking that Jeep and driving back down to Salvador to take the next flight home?'

Her host didn't look remotely perturbed. 'Well,

I'd have to report it as stolen, and the *policia* here are very efficient. So there's really no point.'

The same sense of futility she'd felt in New York sank into Lia's bones as she had to come to terms with the truth smacking her in the face—she was here for the weekend.

As if reading her mind, her host unfolded his arms and held a hand out, gesturing eloquently for her to take his invitation to look around.

Capitulation wasn't easy, but after a few seconds of inner struggle she bent down to slip off her shoes—which were now officially killing her. When she straightened, holding the shoes in her hand, she said tightly, 'As it appears that I have no choice, lead the way.'

Ignoring the fact that she felt a lot more fragile without the added height of her shoes, she followed him deeper into the villa and tried to avert her gaze from that broad back, tapering down to lean hips and tight buttocks.

It was almost a relief to focus on the furnishings, and with some surprise she took in polished wooden floors and open white shutters allowing the warm breeze to circulate. The rooms flowed into each other, the spaces generous and open.

It was casual, yet elegant without being osten-tatious. She noted valuable works of art dotted around the rooms and on the walls. Everything complemented each other. The décor was very much to her own pared-down tastes, which was something she had not expected.

A spacious den was comfortable and inviting, with low coffee tables and a media centre. Huge art and photography books looked well-thumbed, and one wall was shelved and full of books. Her hands itched to explore what was there.

'Your interior designer is very talented,' Lia re-marked.

A dry-sounding, 'Thank you,' made her look at Carter, who had a small smile playing around his mouth. She saw the glint in his eye and then said disbelievingly, 'No... *You* designed this?'

'It's amazing the amount of taste money can buy.'

His tone was even drier now, and there was something else—an edge she'd noticed before, when she'd accused him of being crass. Now she felt uncomfortable. It was disconcerting to feel for the first time as if she was on the back foot.

'It's lovely.'

Wide open French doors led out to the beach. Lia explored a little and her feet sank into deliciously warm and soft sand. The waves of the Atlantic lapped gently and rhythmically against the shore. In spite of herself, something inside her loosened. It had been so long since she'd just…relaxed. Her father's weak health was such a worry, and he depended on her so much…

'Careful,' drawled Benjamin Carter, from too close, 'or I might think you like it here.'

Immediately any sense of relaxation went out of the window and Lia glared at his back as he led her inside again, through a central open courtyard with a pool that was shaded by palm trees.

He showed her a large kitchen, gleamingly pristine with sparkling utensils and a marble worktop. Placing his hands on the counter, where they looked very large and tanned, he said, 'This is Esmé's domain. She's my local housekeeper and chef. She takes care of the place when I'm not here and opens it up for me. She'll be in later to cook dinner.'

Lia dragged her gaze up from those hands and ignored the illicit flutter in her abdomen at the sudden image of a romantic candlelit dinner on the beach. She was silent as she followed him through the villa again and upstairs. Several bedrooms lay off a wide corridor there, with a luxurious runner carpet, and then he walked across a balconied atrium. He opened a door and said, 'This is your room.'

She looked at him suspiciously, and he said with a wide-eyed innocence that she didn't trust for a second, 'What? Did you not think I would be civilised enough to give you your own room? I've told you already—whatever happens will be mutual.'

Lia slipped into the room before he could see her discomfiture. She wasn't used to men being so…up-front. And on some level she wasn't sure *what* she'd expected. One thing she had to admit was that she felt in no danger at all. Her prevailing feeling was that any danger would come from her own reactions.

She dropped her shoes to the floor and walked over to where huge open doors led out to a balcony that looked out on the beach and the sea, just yards away. It was stunning. Just then a small bird flew past, with an iridescent flash of exotic colours. She realised with a sense of irony that the man wouldn't have to resort to any kind of force—this place could seduce a woman all on its own.

When she turned around he gestured. 'There's an en suite bathroom through there, and a dressing room.'

Curious, Lia looked into the massive bathroom. It was gorgeous—with a wet room shower and a huge claw-footed bath. A very feminine part of her sighed in appreciation.

And then through an adjoining door she saw what must be the dressing room. She walked in and gasped when she saw that it was full of clothes, all brand-new, with designer tags still dangling from the expensive fabrics.

Other doors that led back to the main bedroom were pulled open and Benjamin Carter leant nonchalantly against the doorframe, with a faint smile on his face that smacked irritatingly of a man watching a woman having the desired reaction when she saw a closet full of beautiful clothes.

She folded her arms and narrowed her eyes on him, bristling at that look. 'So this is your seduction routine for the women you bring here? Frankly, it takes more than a closet full of expensive clothes to get *my* interest. I'm not that shallow or spoilt—no matter what you might believe.'

Something flashed in his eyes and for a second Lia thought he'd taken offence. He didn't move, but she could sense his tension.

'Actually, I've never brought a woman here before. But I do loan the villa to friends and business acquaintances. I keep the two master suites stocked with clothes because the nearest boutique is in Salvador. A stylist I employ checks the stock after each visit and removes the clothes that have been worn, which are then given to a local charity.'

Lia felt ashamed of her quick judgement. This wasn't like her... But he pushed her buttons like no one else. And had he really never brought a woman here? She tried to read his now expressionless face and had to admit that a man like him wouldn't lie about that. Why would he need to?

The realisation that it must be some sort of sanctuary for him made her feel even more vulnerable. She weakly chose deflection to avoid acknowledging the revelation that she was the first woman he'd brought here.

'Well,' she said stiffly, 'that's very generous of

you, but I've brought my own clothes.' She belatedly realised that her autumn/winter clothes would obviously be totally unsuitable in this climate.

Ben straightened from the door now, and for the first time since she'd met him Lia sensed a slight chill in the air. Contrary to the way she would have expected to feel, she didn't like it.

He glanced at his watch. 'It's my first time here this year, so I have a few maintenance things to catch up on. Make yourself at home. There's plenty of food in the kitchen if you'd like a snack. And you've seen where the beach is—it's entirely private, so you won't be disturbed.'

And then he turned to walk out. A veritable cauldron of emotions rendered Lia immobile and speechless for a moment as she watched him leave. There was anger that he'd all but kidnapped her, but that was fading in light of these all too seductive surroundings and the fact that he was giving her space.

And then she castigated herself for being so easily duped—because he *had* to have an agenda. And she needed to remember that. Because something was shifting, and if she wasn't careful she'd be falling under a spell she might not be able to resist.

She hurried to the door of the bedroom in her bare feet and saw his broad back descending the stairs. 'If this is all just to get to my father then you might as well send me back to New York right now,' she blurted out. 'Because I would never let someone seduce me to get to him.'

Ben stopped in his tracks. Frustration still coursed through his blood. Never had a woman so comprehensively stonewalled him. And certainly not one who wanted him. And never had a woman had such an obviously low opinion of him. To his utter chagrin, when usually he couldn't care less what people thought of him, he found himself caring about her opinion.

She looked at him as if he was something stuck on the bottom of her shoe, even as that pulse beat hectically under her skin at her neck, every time he came close.

Slowly he turned around, jaw tight, teetering on the edge of telling her that he'd arrange for her to be taken back to Salvador, but then he saw her hovering by the doorway, and that compulsion died a death when he saw the expression on her face. There was still defiance, but there was also something he hadn't seen before—a kind of wary uncertainty. A hint of vulnerability. It made him think of the fleeting look of hurt he thought he'd seen when he'd called her a princess. And the moment of sheer terror on her face when her friend had asked her to step in for the model at the charity auction.

In bare feet, and still wearing that decadent dress which was badly creased by now, with her hair loose and mussed around her shoulders after the long journey, she looked more beautiful than anything he'd ever seen in his life.

And he wanted her.

Ben slowly came back up the stairs, seeing how her eyes widened. She was tense, too, and it wasn't just from anger at his commandeering of this situation. She was tense because of him, because she wanted him, and suddenly Ben knew that there was no way he was letting her go.

He stopped a few feet away from her. 'I won't stand here and insult your intelligence by denying that I have an interest in your father's business…but right now I'm not concerned with that.'

Ben was surprised to find that he really wasn't. Right now all his interest was focused on one thing. *Lia.* And making her acquiesce to him.

She swallowed and his eyes tracked the movement down the slim column of her throat.

Finally she said, in those cut-glass tones, 'You won't get anywhere with me, Mr Carter, so I think it would be best if we just kept ourselves to ourselves until it's time to go home.'

Ben almost felt sorry for her as he answered, 'You really shouldn't issue a challenge like that, Lia…'

CHAPTER FOUR

'YOU REALLY SHOULDN'T issue a challenge like that...'

That evening, Benjamin Carter's words still re-sounded in Lia's head. Damn the man.

After pacing her sumptuous room for a couple of hours that morning, she'd finally explored the dressing room. Determined to make the most of this situation, she'd kitted herself out in a modest bathing suit and some beach attire. After helping herself to a light lunch in the kitchen she'd headed to the beach.

There had been no sign of Benjamin Carter, much to her relief, but she had heard some noises that sounded as if they were coming from the front of the house. Not wanting to face him in a diaphanous beach cover-up, she'd found an idyllic spot on the beach under the shade of a palm tree, out of immediate sight of the villa.

For a few hours she had almost fooled herself that she was on a vacation she'd chosen willingly.

She'd dozed, swum, and read a book that she'd pulled off the shelf in the comfortable den.

She'd returned to the villa as dusk was falling and had nearly tripped over her own feet when she'd seen a half-naked Ben Carter perched precariously on the terracotta rooftop of the villa. Her eyes had been immediately drawn to the sleek muscles of his broad back, moving sinuously under his skin as he'd hammered something into a slate.

The fact that he had been laughing and joking with another man, whose ebony skin had also been gleaming with exertion, had gone largely unnoticed. Carter had been wearing nothing but a faded pair of board shorts and battered-looking sneakers.

Lia had almost jumped out of her skin when a melodious and mischievous-sounding voice had said near her ear, 'Not a bad sight at the end of a hot day, hmm?'

She'd looked to her left to see a startlingly pretty young woman, with skin the colour of warm chocolate, eyes to match and a huge smile. With a colourful scarf on her head, she had blended into the exotic background perfectly.

The woman had introduced herself as Esmé, and after explaining that the other man was her husband had said, 'I was just coming to find you. Ben sends his apologies for being busy all afternoon but says he'll look forward to you joining him for dinner at eight.'

Lia had been about to demur when she'd realised she was being ridiculous, and that this nice woman didn't deserve to be put out just because the last person she wanted to have dinner with was her host.

Are you so sure about that? a little voice had crowed.

In any event, Lia had made her escape from the provocative view of a far less civilised Benjamin Carter before he'd been able to turn around and see her reaction, which was confusing to her on so many levels. Since when had she found men doing manual labour particularly enticing? And why did the sight of him doing something so earthy appeal to her so much?

She cursed her revolving thoughts now, as she debated what to wear after her shower. A part of her wanted to wear jeans and a shirt, but then she thought of the mocking look in Carter's eyes when he registered that she was obviously trying *not* to make an effort. So instead she picked out a simple black silk dress that had a scooped neckline and a gathered waist. It fell to her knees. Positively nun-like. Perfect.

After applying a minimum of make-up, and pulling her hair back into a low bun, she slid on her own kitten heel shoes and made her way downstairs, noticing that she was just on time. She was just grumbling to herself that she was pathologically incapable of being late, even if she wanted to be, when Carter appeared in the lobby below, with a bottle of wine in one hand and a glass in the other.

He'd been transformed from manual labourer back to suave, elegant businessman, in dark charcoal-coloured trousers and a light grey shirt. Lia could see that his normally unruly hair looked damp, and was bombarded with an X-rated image of him in a shower, with water sluicing down over those impressive muscles.

'Esmé told me she'd found you. I apologise again for leaving you to your own devices but after Joao—Esmé's husband—offered his services for the afternoon, we managed to get all the maintenance jobs done at once.'

Lia wasn't quite sure how she'd made it down the stairs, but now she was standing only a few feet away from him. Something about his easy manner and her sense of this villa feeling far too familiar, even after such a short time, was very disconcerting.

Her voice was husky. 'I wasn't expecting you to entertain me. I had a lovely afternoon on the beach.'

His voice had a faintly disbelieving tone. 'You weren't bored?'

Lia shook her head, realising that the afternoon had been far more pleasant than she'd even admitted to herself. And if she *had* felt a tiny sense of loneliness it hadn't been for the company of this man, she assured herself fiercely, and got a grip on her wayward emotions. She put it down to the after-effects of the sun.

'I swam and read a book. I haven't had a chance to do that for a long time.'

He didn't respond, but Lia could imagine that Carter believed she meant since her last luxury holiday. She bit back the urge to disabuse him of that notion. She didn't care what his opinion of her was... All that mattered was putting up with this weekend for the sake of his charitable donation.

Lia followed him into the salon, where the lights had been dimmed and candles flickered invitingly. The air was still warm after the day, and it was heavenly after the biting breeze of autumn in New York.

Carter turned from where he was opening some wine at a drinks cabinet. 'Would you like a glass? It's from a good friend's vineyard in Argentina.'

Lia was about to say no, but then something stopped her. A rogue desire to give in to this seductive relaxation. So she nodded and took the glass of chilled white wine, noticing that Ben Carter had picked up a glass of what looked like water. She recalled that he hadn't ordered alcohol on their date—or *non*-date. And he hadn't been drinking at the charity auction.

'You don't drink?' she heard herself asking, before she could stop the words.

He shook his head and gestured for her to take a seat on the couch behind her. He sat on another couch, on the other side of the coffee table, his arm spread across the back, his big body dominating the space easily.

Lia looked away and took a sip of wine. It slid down her throat like cool silk, its bouquet flooding her senses and making her head instantly light. And even though she wasn't looking at him his image was burned into her retinas. He reminded Lia of a lounging pasha she'd seen once in a painting, surrounded by a bevy of exotic beauties. The civilised surroundings didn't diminish his robust masculinity at all. And that provocative memory of him half-naked wasn't helping.

He eventually supplied, 'I don't drink. At all.'

She couldn't keep averting her gaze, so she looked back to see that his expression was almost challenging. She just shrugged, as if her curiosity wasn't as piqued as it was. 'I don't drink much myself...a couple of glasses is usually my limit.'

Some of the tension seemed to go out of his shoulders. The thought of him having had a drink problem... She just couldn't see it. He was way too in control. Perhaps it had something to do with his upbringing?

Just then Esmé appeared at the entrance of the room and told them dinner was served. Ben stood and let Lia precede him out of the room to the dining room next door, similarly dimly lit, with candles flickering.

A table was set with a white tablecloth and silver. It was very romantic. And that, along with her sudden curiosity to know more about this man, made Lia say stiffly, 'You really shouldn't have gone to this trouble.'

He held out Lia's chair and she had to sit down, very aware of him behind her.

As he came around and took his own seat he drawled, 'It took an eight-hour plane journey and a two-hour time difference to get you to have dinner with me, so a little effort is worth it, I think.'

Lia looked at him and had to figure that most men wouldn't have bothered pursuing her this far—or they would be resenting the trouble they'd gone to. A man she'd dated briefly before her ex-fiancé had turned nasty when she'd been less than eager to jump into bed after their first date. It was one of the reasons she'd liked Simon—because he'd respected her boundaries. Little had she known that he was being respectful because he was eyeing up a chance to get a permanent foothold in the legal team who represented her father's company, and because his 'needs' were being met elsewhere.

But Carter was still here, and it felt as if he had stormed into her life, blasting apart the cynicism she'd built around herself after her parents' break-up and her disastrous engagement.

The consequences if she was to unbend even slightly and give in to his seduction were suddenly terrifying to contemplate—because Lia knew now that he'd already slid under her skin enough to make an impact that she really didn't want to acknowledge.

For him this was just about a conquest—personal and professional. Of that she had no doubt.

She leaned forward slightly. 'Look, Mr Carter... I know that this is about my father as much as you say it's about me—'

But she had to stop as Esmé appeared with their starters—beautifully prepared individual ravioli in a cream and mushroom sauce. Lia didn't miss the all-too-interested look the woman sent to each of them.

When they were alone again he responded. 'First of all, my name is Ben. Second of all, the fact that I have a professional interest in your father is common knowledge. Many others have—not just me. Your father has never had a problem protecting his interests, so unless something has changed he is perfectly safe, no matter what happens between us. And thirdly…when I saw your photo in the matchmaker's portfolio I wanted you before I knew who you were.'

The words sat between them in the thick silence. Fatally, all Lia registered was that he'd wanted her before he'd known who she was. And, God help her, that struck deep. It was like when she'd been standing on that dais and someone had wanted her enough to bid a small fortune for her…an elusive stranger she'd thought she wanted. Who was *him*. The man sitting across from her now, blue eyes glinting. Handsome as sin.

This man was dangerous to her because he made her yearn for things she'd thought she could live without—for deeply personal desires to be fulfilled. For a man to touch her and make her come alive. Prove to her that she wasn't defective in some way…

And then she thought of what he'd said about her father. The truth was that her father *was* vulnerable—he needed to retire and there was no one he trusted enough to take over the business. Lia realised that she was leading Carter to question her father's robustness when she should be taking the opportunity to deflect it.

She had to give a little…or he'd smell blood.

She forced herself to relax slightly and sucked in a breath. 'Fine. Ben it is.' Her heart thumped as she said his name. It felt ridiculously intimate.

He held out his hand across the table, over their fragrant starters. 'Truce?'

Lia reluctantly held out her own hand. 'Truce.'

His hand enveloped hers and she had a flashback to seeing him on the roof, skin gleaming with exertion, those muscles bunching and moving. She tried to pull her hand back but his fingers tightened and an unmistakable fire in his eyes mesmerised her.

'I'm glad you're here, Lia,' he said. 'I look forward to getting to know you better.'

Ben didn't fool himself for a second that Lia's apparent acquiescence had anything to do with *him*, per se. Oh, she wanted him—that was obvious. But she was still determined to fight it. Still, after he'd declared that truce, and resisted the urge to pull her over the table towards him so he could kiss her, they'd actually had a cordial meal and conversed. Albeit about completely superficial subjects.

On one level it infuriated Ben, because he knew now that he'd underestimated her hugely, and yet she seemed to be determined to close him off, not let him see beneath the surface. And he only had himself to blame. For a man not used to failure—in anything—it was disconcerting.

They'd finished dinner now, and she'd joined him back in the living area for coffee. She was walking around the room, looking at pictures and books, cradling her coffee cup in her hand.

Without that direct blue gaze assessing his every movement, Ben could look his fill. The dress she wore was lovely, but it comprehensively covered her body. He guessed she'd chosen it for that very reason, and once again he found her reluctance to give in to the chemistry between them slightly mystifying.

He didn't think that any of her reluctance to come with him had been feigned, so he knew she wasn't the kind of woman who would play hard to get. And yet he'd never expend this much effort on a woman who didn't want him, so it made him wonder about her, about her experience. Maybe he'd underestimated her in more ways than one?

He asked carefully, 'So, in light of the fact that you'd signed up with Leviathan Solutions, I'm a little curious as to why you seemed so eager to leave it after your first date?'

He saw how her whole body stiffened at that question. She turned around slowly, after putting the book she'd been looking at back on the shelf. He saw her clear reluctance to speak on her face and it fascinated him—he was used to women who had injected so much filler that they couldn't emote more than a tense smile.

After a long moment when he thought she was going to deflect his question, she said tightly, 'The truth is that I had no desire to join a dating agency. Someone decided to do it on my behalf.'

Ben's curiosity shot up, but he schooled his expression. 'Who would do such a thing?'

She sighed and came and sat down. Every move she made exuded that effortless casual elegance, even when she was tense.

She put her cup down and looked at Ben. 'It was

my father's idea. He's old-fashioned, and he's determined to see me settled.'

She shut her mouth, as if she'd said too much. Ben could see that she was tempted to fold her arms, shut him out completely. It suddenly occurred to him as he took in her vaguely tortured expression…and when he recalled her reaction to, and subsequent tension during the charity auction…that she might actually be *shy*.

He leant forward. 'I know you're not gay—not after that kiss we shared… So what is it, Lia? Why don't you want to date?'

She stood up again, agitated, and moved back over to the shelves, turning to face him. 'Is it so hard to believe that a woman might not want her life to revolve around a man? That she might have ambitions of her own? In case you hadn't heard, a revolution was fought and won a long time ago.'

Ben sat back, more and more intrigued by these buttons he was pushing. He drawled, 'I'm no misogynist, Lia, and some would say there's still a fight to be fought. But people—women in particular—can multitask, dating and working at the same time.'

Now she flushed. 'I know that.' She wrapped her

arms around herself. 'I just… My father shouldn't have done that. Not after—'

She broke off abruptly and Ben sat forward again. 'After what?'

She glanced away, her jaw tight. When she looked at him again after a moment, she said, 'Well, it's not as if you couldn't find out easily enough.' She lifted her chin. 'I was engaged briefly. A year ago.'

'Who was he?' Ben asked sharply, hackles rising.

Lia came back around the couch and sat down, picking up her coffee again. 'I met him at one of my father's parties. He was a solicitor with a firm that my father's legal team uses sometimes to take on extra work.'

Ben felt a surge of that same possessiveness he'd experienced when he'd seen Lia standing on that dais in front of everyone. 'I wouldn't have had you down as the wife of a mere lackey.'

Lia's eyes sparked. 'No? That just shows how much you don't know about me, doesn't it?'

Ben shrugged a shoulder. 'I hardly know you, Lia, but I know you're more than just corporate wife material. He would have stifled you to death.'

It surprised him that he *did* know this. And it made him wonder what on earth kind of marriage of convenience *he* had in mind, if not corporate.

He noticed then how she'd gone still. 'That's some leap to make when you hardly know me...'

Ben grimaced. 'I owe you an apology. I was wrong about you. You're not a princess, Lia. If you were you'd have been screaming and begging to get back to civilisation hours ago, and yet you've been perfectly happy here all day, looking after yourself. Esmé told me you made your lunch and cleaned up after yourself.'

She responded with a touch of wry defensiveness. 'Making lunch and cleaning up hardly merits special congratulations. I've still had a more privileged upbringing than most people ever see in their lifetimes.'

'But you're not spoilt. Far from it.'

For a long time she said nothing, biting her lip. And then, finally, 'No, not as you might have imagined at first. It's been just my father and I since my parents divorced. I became his hostess from a young age and...and I think he overcompensated to make up for the separation. But I was never really comfortable with lavish gifts or things like that. Once he was happy, *I* was happy.'

Ben absorbed this nugget, acknowledging uncomfortably that he'd misjudged her again. He'd known Louis Ford was divorced, but not the particulars. He asked, 'Where's your mother now?'

Lia shrugged minutely and her face was carefully expressionless. Ben recognised it because he used that defence mechanism himself when someone asked too many questions about his past.

'I think she's in a Swiss château with husband number four. It's hard to pin Estella down. I don't see her often. When I was a teenager she would summon me periodically to whatever luxurious resort she was residing in at the time, usually when she was between husbands and in need of distraction.'

Ben felt a surge of irritation at this faceless woman, but he said lightly, 'She sounds charming.'

Lia blinked at Ben and then put down her cup and stood up abruptly, taking him by surprise. He'd not even noticed that they'd got into a personal discussion, and he usually did his utmost to avoid straying into such territory with women.

He stood up too, just as she said, 'It's been a long day. I think I'll go to bed.'

'Of course.' His gaze tracked her as she turned to leave the room, and then he made a split-second decision and said, 'I thought that perhaps tomorrow I could give you a tour of Salvador. It's a stunning city, and I'd like to make it up to you for leaving you to your own devices today.'

She stopped, and the lines of her body were tense. For a moment Ben had a premonition that she was going to turn around and say enough was enough, that she wanted to go home tomorrow… And in all conscience he realised that he couldn't really say no if she wanted to. Even as everything in him rejected the thought.

But she turned quickly and just said, 'Okay— fine.'

And then she was disappearing from view and Ben let out a long breath, more relieved by that small concession than anything he could recall in a long time.

As soon as Lia made it back to her room she closed the door and leant back against it, breathing deeply to calm her racing heart. What the hell had just happened down there? She'd been moments away from curling up on the couch and spilling her entire guts to Benjamin Carter, as if he was some kind of confidant she could trust.

It had only been when he'd responded to what she'd revealed about her mother, and she'd had the distinct impression that he was angry on her behalf, that she'd snapped back to reality. First of all, she never spoke about her mother to anyone—the old wound of rejection still smarted, and she usually avoided being drawn into any discussion about it. *Usually.*

And what about telling him that she wasn't interested in dating? And letting him provoke her into talking about her failed engagement?

Lia groaned and kicked off her shoes, walking over to the French doors that led out to the balcony.

The air was still deliciously warm and balmy, caressing her bare skin. She couldn't see anything in the inky darkness but she could hear the gentle lap of waves against the shore and it soothed her jittery nerves a little, and her sense of exposure.

She thought of his apologising for calling her a princess, and his observation that she was more than corporate wife material, and something inside her felt weak. And yet hadn't she almost settled for that? Because after yet another stroke, her concern for her father's health had been so great that she'd given in to his plea that she give Simon Barnes—the nice but dull solicitor—a chance.

When she'd started dating him and they'd had a frank discussion he'd admitted that he'd pursued her to get into her father's good graces, thus potentially securing a job on his legal team. Simon had then assured her that he would not stand in the way of her ambitions, and so—foolishly, maybe—Lia had seen a way to keep her father happy, and also to forge a life for herself within a marriage that wouldn't confine her.

After all, she'd never entertained romantic notions of a happy-ever-after marriage—not after witnessing her own parents' disastrous marriage and her father's subsequent heartbreak. Lia had vowed from an early age never to be so destroyed by giving someone else that control over her.

But then her chest grew tight when she recalled that oh, so vivid image of her fiancé's head buried between his secretary's legs, and the humiliation washed over her again. It hadn't been his infidelity that had hurt her—after all, they hadn't been in love—it had been the stark knowledge of the fact that *she* hadn't been able to rouse that passion in him.

Lia curled her hands around the balcony railings as if that would centre her again. The truth was that as much as she wished she could find it easy to dismiss Benjamin Carter...she couldn't.

Something about this place, about *him*, was making her loosen up. Dangerously so. She'd all but accused him of being boorish and she had outright accused him of being crass. But this beautiful house didn't belong to a crass man, and a boorish man didn't climb up to hammer slates into a roof with his housekeeper's husband. And, an overly arrogant man who had made no bones about the fact that he wanted to take her to bed wouldn't exercise such restraint that he'd actually let her go to bed. Alone.

Lia hadn't mistaken the heat in his eyes... It was one of the reasons, apart from her over-sharing, that she'd practically run from the room.

She had to remind herself that the man was a consummate playboy; he knew exactly what he was doing. He was like a big jungle cat playing with a tiny helpless mouse—letting it believe that it could get away when all he had to do was bring down a big paw and that would be that. Game over.

She'd been here less than twenty-four hours and the man was already playing her like a fiddle. Lia was very tempted to go back downstairs and demand that he take her home immediately.

Funnily enough, she suspected that if she insisted he would let her go. But, perversely, she didn't want to give him the satisfaction, or let him suspect for a second that she was perturbed by all that she'd revealed to him. One more day in his company… She could keep her mouth zipped and keep him at a distance. She could. She had to.

Lia sat beside Ben in the open-top Jeep as they drove down the main route to Salvador from his villa. Her dark hair was pulled back into a practical ponytail and the warm breeze made it look like skeins of silk behind her head. He was finding it hard to maintain some semblance of control. It was as if he'd never seen a woman dressed in a sleeveless T-shirt and shorts before. But he'd never seen *this* woman dressed like that before, and it was all he could do not to stop and ogle her slender pale limbs.

She seemed ethereal and delicate beside him. Even though he knew he shouldn't be thinking of her as delicate at all. When she'd arrived in the kitchen earlier she'd had a determined look on her face and had kept up a general patter of inane conversation. No doubt signalling to Ben that the little confidences of the previous evening wouldn't be happening again.

And that the sooner this weekend was over the better.

In fact—and his jaw clenched when he thought of it now—she seemed to be determined to treat him as if he was just a hired tour guide. Bestowing bright smiles upon him and sticking to annoyingly trite and inconsequential conversation.

Determined to crack through that cheerfully icy veneer, Ben asked, 'So, did you sleep well?'

The dark glasses she wore hid her eyes, and when Ben glanced at her she was smiling brightly. 'I slept like a log, thank you. All this fresh sea air makes such a change from muggy city pollution.'

His jaw clenched again. Time to ruffle her feathers a little. 'Aren't you going to ask how *I* slept?'

She looked at him, and he could sense the glare behind those protective shades. 'I hadn't planned on it, no.'

'Well, if you must know,' he said, 'I didn't sleep well at all. Lots of tossing and turning.' He grimaced. 'And I had to take a shower during the night.'

Because every time he'd closed his eyes all he'd been able to envisage was an image of her, standing in her long red evening dress, looking crumpled but sexily dishevelled, and he'd wondered what it would have been like to go and pick her up and bring her into his bedroom—

'Well,' she said stiffly now, her faux brightness gone, 'we didn't *have* to do this today. You know, if you're too tired, you can always drop me off at the airport and I can get a flight home. That way you can get as much rest as you need.'

His mouth quirked. 'Not a chance. And I didn't say I was tired. I don't sleep much, as a general rule.'

She was practically bristling beside him now.

He continued, 'So, tell me about these ambitions of yours…the ones you mentioned last night when you were assuring me that a woman's life doesn't have to revolve around a man.'

She crossed her arms and stared straight ahead. 'I don't think that's any business of yours.'

'Maybe not,' he agreed, glancing across at her, his eye instantly caught by the lush curve of her mouth. 'But humour me?'

Damn the man, Lia thought churlishly. She'd bet money he was just trying to rile her. And her sense of complacency had gone out of the window as soon as he'd revealed that he'd taken a shower during the night.

It had been hard enough to maintain a cool front as soon as she'd walked into the kitchen and seen him sprawled in a chair, wearing faded worn jeans and a dark polo shirt, with bare feet.

His hair had still been wet and he'd looked at her over his coffee cup and said, 'You should have joined me for a swim in the sea this morning. It was magnificent.'

Instantly Lia had been bombarded with an image of their wet bodies entwined as waves crashed around them.

She'd forced a sunny smile and sat down, helping herself to coffee and ignoring his comment. 'It's almost hard to believe we were in New York this time yesterday, isn't it?'

Until now she'd kept up her valiant façade.

'Tell me about these ambitions of yours...'

Lia thought about his question for a long moment. This was exactly what she'd reassured herself she'd do last night—keep him at a distance. Get on a plane and go home. And yet...there was something inside her that felt as if it wanted to break free.

It might be the sun-drenched exotic surroundings and the sense of being out of her comfort zone, thanks to having been literally transported to another country. Or it might be the effort it was taking to resist this man's natural charm. Or, more dangerously, it might be the desire to reveal herself. Somehow along the way his opinion had come to matter to her—just a tiny bit.

She sighed volubly and Ben said cajolingly from beside her, 'It's another thirty minutes to Salvador...'

Treacherously, she felt resistance give way inside her. Angry with herself for giving in she said almost accusingly, 'If you must know, I studied Architectural Engineering at university.'

It was almost worth saying that to see the way his head snapped around.

Lia smiled sweetly. 'Didn't expect that, did you?'

Ben had the grace to look slightly sheepish and he said, 'When I met with your father at your house a few years ago he said you were on a skiing trip...'

Lia rolled her eyes. 'I've never skied in my life. I was in college. My father never liked to admit to anyone—or himself—that his daughter had ambitions and wanted a career. He preferred people to think I was a harmless socialite.'

Ben's jaw clenched and Lia saw his hands tighten on the steering wheel.

'I have to confess that I did assume you were part of a certain social set...'

Something tightened in Lia's chest. 'I guess that's understandable. Most people aren't interested in my qualifications.'

He glanced at her before looking back at the road. Lia was glad his eyes were covered. She wasn't sure if she wanted to see what was in them.

'So, what do you plan to do with your degree?'

She hesitated for a moment, and then said, 'I have a specific interest in crisis zones—in being the first on the ground to help with the rebuild.'

'Hence your interest in the charity whose benefit we were attending? They're renowned for the work they do in desperate situations.'

She nodded. 'I volunteered with them after an earthquake in South East Asia, and that's when I became really committed. I persuaded my father to support the charity too.'

Ben cast her another quick look, a wry tilt to his mouth. 'You weren't planning on shopping this weekend, were you?'

Lia shook her head, her heart tripping at the thought that she was telling him this. 'No, I had planned to go to a series of lectures at NYU.'

He said with a devilish grin, 'I'd be lying if I said I was sorry for upsetting your plans.'

Lia felt breathless again as something hot moved through her. Then Ben made a small whistling sound.

'Intelligent, noble *and* beautiful? If you're trying to turn me off, it's not working.'

Lia felt a rush of pride and berated herself for

being so weak as to seek his regard. But still…
The fact that he seemed to be so accepting of this
more secret side to her meant something.

In a bid to deflect attention from her, she said,
'The CEO of that charity appeared to know you?'

He nodded. 'Believe it or not, I'm also interested in what it takes to make disaster areas stable
again. I've taken equipment and some of my men
into crisis zones to help them stabilise buildings,
the infrastructure. The truth is I'm one of the patrons of that charity.'

His words sank in and Lia turned in her seat to
face him, shocked. Instant humiliation washed
over her, because she'd believed he'd pursued her
there for no other reason than to get her to agree to
date him. *Because he'd wanted her so badly.* Now
she felt like an abject fool—because he would
have been there anyway.

Had he simply seen her there and made the most
of the opportunity? More humiliation flooded her
when she thought of how she'd just been laying
out her accomplishments, seeking his approval.
Lord, she had it bad.

Fury strangled her words, but eventually she
got out, 'Stop the car—*now.*'

She had her hand on the door handle even before Ben pulled the car into a layby. As soon as it stopped she jumped out and faced him when he got out too and stood beside the bonnet. She pushed her sunglasses on top of her head and put her hands on her hips, not even sure why she was so angry...just that she was.

'So everyone there must have known exactly who you were, and yet you let me make a complete fool of myself—standing on that podium with no clue as to who on earth you were—'

He came towards her, cutting her off. 'My aim was never to make a fool of you, Lia. I hadn't intended on hiding my identity for as long as I did.'

He muttered something that sounded like a curse and pushed his own sunglasses to his head. His eyes were intense on her, making her regret reacting so forcefully.

Ben went on. 'The opportunity to talk to you without you knowing who I was was too tempting. Especially after that date. And the truth is that I didn't want to see your reaction when you realised who you'd been talking to.'

Lia forced down the weak way she wanted to seize on that and folded her arms. 'That doesn't change the fact that you saw me and made the most of an opportunity. Were you bored? Was that it? You thought you'd have some fun at my expense?'

Ben frowned and shook his head. 'No, it wasn't like that at all. I had no plans to go to that particular function, Lia. I went because I found out that was where you'd be.'

The fire drained out of Lia's anger like a stealthy traitor. She believed him. He looked almost angry, as if he hadn't wanted to admit this to her. A muscle pulsed in his jaw.

Lia was embarrassed by the emotion she'd shown even as she began to feel mollified. She'd revealed far too much. So she just said, 'Okay,' and walked back to the car and got in.

Ben looked at her for a long moment as she buckled up, and then he got in too. For the remainder of their journey to Salvador they only spoke when Ben pointed out things of interest to Lia.

The fact that they *did* share a common interest in a cause very close to Lia's heart was something that she'd never expected, and it wasn't doing much to help her resolve to keep him at a distance.

CHAPTER FIVE

'THIS IS ONE of the earliest squares in Salvador, laid out by the then governor. And that is the Catedral Basílica de São Salvador—one of the most ornately decorated baroque churches in Brazil.'

Lia had thought she couldn't be more impressed than she already was, but as she followed Ben into the huge church off the beautiful square and saw how everything gleamed with gold—literally—her jaw dropped. She had to hand it to him for keeping this till last.

It was a fitting end to what she had to admit had been a very enjoyable day—after that skirmish by the side of the road.

Almost against her will Lia had found herself relaxing bit by bit as Ben showed her around the stunning city which had once been next in importance to Lisbon in the Portuguese colony. It was vibrantly colourful, with hilly cobbled streets and baroque architecture everywhere, and she'd been charmed from the start.

Everyone seemed to smile all the time, and the mix of cultures and nationalities—many of the population were descended from African slaves—added to the melting pot atmosphere. There was music everywhere, calling to a side of Lia that she didn't indulge often.

Just as she'd relaxed when she'd sunk her feet into the sand outside Ben's villa yesterday, something seemed to be unwinding inside her today. Everything about this place called on her to settle into a different rhythm. It was intoxicating. And Ben, surprisingly, was a brilliant guide. A natural storyteller.

He'd also proved himself to be a consummate gentleman. If he'd touched her at all it had been only fleetingly, to draw her attention to something—like when they'd stood on a bluff overlooking the city and the impressive bay. Perversely, that had seemed to have more of an effect on her than if he'd touched her with more intent.

He'd taken her to lunch to an admittedly dubious-looking restaurant on the seafront earlier. Catching her expression, he had chided softly,

'Don't let its exterior fool you—the owner keeps it looking like this to scare the tourists away. This place serves the best fish in Brazil, and it's for locals only.'

He'd been right. To Lia's surprise it had been pristine inside, and the fish had indeed been the best she'd ever tasted, served on a beautiful rooftop with trellised vines keeping the harshness of the sun at bay. The smell of the sea had only added to the taste.

She was acutely aware of Ben now, as he walked close behind her as they looked around the cathedral.

Lia stopped at the wooden altar, which was covered in a thin layer of gold. She shook her head. 'This is totally over the top, but it's beautiful.'

'I know.'

She glanced up to see Ben had come to stand beside her and was looking up at the ceiling. He said, 'They brought the stone for a lot of these buildings all the way from Portugal, on ships. The sheer industry involved is breathtaking.'

Lia hardly heard what he said. She was mesmerised by the strong column of his throat and that proud profile. The sensual curve of his fuller lower lip. She wondered about his early life. Where exactly had he dragged himself from to become such a titan of industry?

Just then someone bumped into her from behind, making her pitch forward into thin air, but within a split-second strong arms were around her and she was pressed close to Ben's side as he accepted someone's profuse apology over her head.

Lia's breasts were crushed against hard muscle, and every curve she had and even some she hadn't been aware of melted into Ben's form as if they'd just been waiting for this opportunity. Her hands were splayed across his chest and she was very aware of the thin material of his T-shirt. She'd noticed how it had moulded to those defined muscles whenever the breeze had caught it during the day. And the way his faded jeans clung lovingly to powerful thighs and tight buttocks.

For someone who up till now hadn't considered herself very sexual, some switch seemed to have been well and truly turned to *on*.

The tour group behind them moved on but Ben didn't release her. She was filled with lassitude and a reluctance to break free. Slowly she looked up—and fell straight into those bluer-than-blue eyes.

The memory of that hot kiss in New York emblazoned itself on her mind…she wanted to reach up and feel his mouth on hers again. Feel the slick slide of his tongue against hers. Something sizzled.

'I'm okay…' Lia finally managed to get out, pulling herself back from the brink of humiliating herself again. 'You can let me go now.'

For a moment Ben didn't, and Lia's heart spasmed with anticipation in the flickering glow of a thousand candles, and then he did, saying with a little grimace, 'As my thoughts are decidedly *un*holy right now, I think it's for the best.'

By the time they'd reached the entrance again and walked out, with Lia keeping a careful few steps behind Ben, she'd almost got herself under control. She'd just had a glimpse of how much he'd lulled her into a false sense of security, but instead of making her angry, she felt excited.

The setting sun was burnishing everything with blazing orange and pink, and some musicians nearby were infusing the air with a contagious tropical beat. An old Bahian couple danced together and for a moment Lia felt reckless, giddy. Just as she had on the dais at the auction… *Dangerous*. Maybe the intense smell of incense had got to her inside the cathedral? Maybe it was all part of this man's plan to break down her defences until she was just a weak, pliable mess?

Then he turned to look at her and every coherent thought left her head. She already was a weak mess. Pathetic.

Ben frowned then and plucked his phone out of his jeans pocket, looking at the screen. Lia hadn't heard a sound, so it must be on silent, and she only realised then how much attention he'd devoted to her all day, rarely looking at his phone at all—which, in this day of digital over-connectivity, was pretty amazing. Especially for an important CEO of his own company.

Her ex-fiancé, who'd had a far less important job, had always been glued to his *two* phones.

Ben looked at her. 'That was from a friend of mine who lives here in town. He's heard that I'm here and he's invited me to a party in his house tonight.'

Lia felt an acute sense of disappointment that

their day was at an end and, terrified by that re-action, said quickly, 'Oh…of course you should go. I'm sure I can take a bus or a taxi back to the villa…'

He shook his head at her and his eyes gleamed. 'I don't intend to go alone.'

Lia flushed with a mix of pleasure and trepi-dation. Her feelings for this man had undergone a seismic change in just one day—helped by the seductive surroundings, yes, but also because he was proving to be far more enticing than she'd expected.

She'd thought it would be easy to dismiss him. To maintain her aloofness. But right now she was hot and sticky on the outside, and inside, in secret places. Although she had the sense to know that she was no real match for a man like Ben Carter, connoisseur of women. Playboy.

'I couldn't intrude, but you should go.'

Ben shook his head and asked softly, 'When was the last time you did something spontane-ous and had fun?'

The question was so unexpected that Lia blinked for a moment. A kind of cold horror swept through her as she realised that she'd couldn't remember the last really spontaneous thing she'd done. If she'd ever done anything. And as for fun…? She'd had fun with her father on their sailing trips, but they hadn't done one of those for a long time.

As Louis Ford's daughter, not a lot of her colleagues saw her as someone to have fun with when she was keeping an eye on things for her father—no doubt afraid she'd report back to the boss. And, her relationship with Simon certainly hadn't been fun.

Absurdly, she felt her throat grow tight as the pathetic reality sank in. And through it all Ben just watched her with those bright blue eyes, seeing all the way through to where she was most vulnerable.

Lia fought to regain her composure and swallowed the lump in her throat. 'Well, if you're sure he won't mind…'

'He won't.'

Ben smiled, and it knocked the breath from Lia's chest.

'You'll see how things work here—it's much more relaxed. It's not just Luis, it's his husband, Ricardo, too. They love being surrounded by beauty—including beautiful women, so I'll soon be relegated to the sidelines.'

Something inside her contracted at his easy mention of these friends. And the truth was that she wanted to know more about Ben Carter—she couldn't deny it, much as she might want to.

She pointed vaguely at her attire, dusty and wrinkled after the long day, and said ruefully, 'I'm hardly dressed for polite company.'

'I know a place that'll look after us.'

Ben held out his hand. Lia looked at it for a long moment, and then an overwhelming sense of *rightness* made her put her hand in his. He held it as they left the square behind and walked back to the car. And Lia tried to ignore the sensation that she'd just turned a corner and she'd never find her way back.

But she couldn't. It sat in her belly like a fizzing time bomb.

Ben had taken Lia to a friend's boutique after she'd put her hand in his and let him lead her back to the car. Her agreement to go to the party with him had left him buoyant. Crazy how each tiny concession from this woman felt like a ridiculous triumph.

When they'd got to the boutique Ben had tensed, waiting for Lia to turn up her nose at the discreet name over the door, but she'd gone in, oblivious to his tension, showing him yet another facet of her personality—she obviously wasn't defined by designer labels.

Within minutes he'd explained what they needed to Gaby, Esmé's cousin and the shop's owner, and she'd handed Ben some clothes and whisked Lia out of sight behind a swathe of velvet material. Ben waited now, having changed into smart black trousers and a shirt.

When he heard a noise behind him he turned around and for a second his brain froze. Lia stood before him in bare feet, her hair tumbling around her shoulders. And her dress…her dress took his breath away.

It was a long silk wraparound dress in a deep royal blue colour that made her eyes pop like two gems. He could see a tantalising slit in the material that revealed one long shapely leg. He could see even from where he stood that in the space of two days her skin had taken on a faint golden glow, and he knew that there was already a spread of light freckles across her nose.

He felt robbed of breath. As if someone had punched him.

The vee neckline of the dress was a tantalising enticement to pull the material aside. It would be so easy to expose a lush breast and then cup its weight—

Lia started to turn away, saying, 'I knew it. It's too—'

Her voice cut through the haze in his brain. 'No!' His voice sounded too harsh to his ears.

She turned around again, slowly. Amazingly, she looked unsure.

'It's perfect,' he managed to say, sounding only half coherent.

Gaby appeared then, and caught the end of their conversation. 'Ben's right! It's just perfect for one of Ricardo and Luis's parties. And on you, my darling, it is *perfeito*. Come, let's find you some shoes to wear.'

Ben was glad of a moment alone to gather his wits again. What the hell was wrong with him? He'd seen plenty of women in far less clothing and it had never made him feel as if he was teetering on the brink of some kind of meltdown. And usually seeing women in clothes he'd bought them came *after* he'd slept with them.

So far his relationship with Lia was the most chaste he'd ever indulged in. He wasn't necessarily proud to admit that, for him, relationships with women were less about really getting to know them and more about slaking the desire he felt for them, which was usually fleeting.

He had a sense that where Lia was concerned his lust wouldn't be so easily slaked.

For the first time he had to wonder if he'd done the right thing, bringing her here… But then she emerged again, wearing strappy silver sandals, and that last thought was blasted apart by another surge of desire.

He instructed Gaby to put all the items on his tab and took the bag she gave him containing the clothes they'd been wearing earlier. Outside, Ben opened the car door for Lia to get in. He could see her biting her lip, looking concerned.

She stopped with her hand on the door and looked at him. 'I'll pay you back for the clothes.'

Confirmation of the fact that she wasn't spoilt. Another blow to Ben's misconceptions.

'Don't worry about it,' he said gruffly.

Lia slid into the passenger seat, her dress gaping slightly as she did so, affording him a glimpse of the curve of one perfectly rounded breast encased in delicate lace.

Gritting his jaw, Ben closed the door and strode around the other side of the car, praying for the strength to restrain himself. He'd never needed it more than right now.

Ben's friends were an exuberant couple who swept Lia into their embraces and their stunning baroque mansion, high on a hill overlooking the entire city, within seconds. Much to her amusement, Ben had predicted their reaction accurately: he was all but ignored as they grilled her.

'But where have you been all our lives?'

'This is a scandal! You can't live in cold, grey England—move here! We need more beautiful women!'

In truth, they were a little overwhelming, both at once, and soon Ben took advantage of more guests arriving, skilfully manoeuvring them to where long tables covered in pristine white linen groaned under the weight of more food than Lia had ever seen in her life.

Every delicacy was available. and she found herself gravitating towards the local fare, much to the chef's obvious pleasure, as he explained exactly what everything was.

Ben took their plates and Lia picked up their drinks. He guided her over to one of the many small round tables laid out for guests to eat at with ease. It was idyllic, with hundreds of candles flickering and the sparkling lights of the city below them. A jazz band played on a dais in the corner.

After they'd eaten a little, Ben sat back. 'You can admit it—you won't self-combust, I promise.'

She looked at him and knew instantly what he meant. A small, slightly smug smile was playing around that far too gorgeous mouth and something inside her just...*melted*. Also, far more disturbingly, that giddy reckless feeling was back. In the white shirt, open at the neck, he was astonishingly handsome. And the fact that he hadn't pushed her was working in his favour. Damn him.

She picked up a small morsel of cheese from her plate and threw it at him, saying grudgingly,

'Fine. Yes, I'll admit it. I'm glad I came to the party and I'm enjoying myself.'

He flicked the cheese off his shoulder and leaned towards her. 'It's polite to say thank you, you know.'

She could read very well in his expression how he might suggest being thanked, and for a second Lia desperately wished she had the confidence to pull him closer, so she could explore that mouth… She snapped her gaze back up to his, feeling hot. The thought made a spike of pleasure arrow between her legs, and she said, far too breathily, 'Don't push it, Ben.'

He just looked at her for a long moment. 'I won't…for now.'

And right then Lia's belly swooped, because in all honesty she wasn't sure if she could hold him back for much longer. Or if she wanted to.

'He's quite a specimen, isn't he?'

Lia jumped, and blushed when she realised that she'd been spotted ogling Ben—who was standing head and shoulders above everyone else in the crowd—by one of their hosts, Ricardo. The impressive sight of Ben had stalled her momentarily.

The handsome grey-haired Italian who she'd discovered owned several of Brazil's most luxurious hotels was looking at her now, assessingly.

'I...yes, I guess he's handsome,' Lia said weakly.

The other man snorted inelegantly. '*Cara*, he's certifiably one of the sexiest men on the planet, and right now I am jealous of *you*.'

Lia hid her discomfiture and smiled. 'Better not let Luis hear you say that.'

Ricardo waved a dismissive hand. 'Lusting after someone isn't a crime.'

Lia was curious now. 'How do you two know Ben?'

'Oh, we've known Ben since he started out, more or less. When he first set up his company we were among his first clients. We've always been interested in fresh new talent, and we'd seen some of his work in Manhattan. It's really amazing what he's achieved, considering the fact that he was once heir to one of America's biggest fortunes.'

Lia frowned. 'What do you mean?'

He looked at her, incredulous. 'You don't know?'

'Know what?'

Ricardo looked at her as if she'd grown two

heads. 'Ben was born into American royalty—more or less. His father was Jonathan Carter, the man who practically owned Wall Street until it was revealed that he'd been defrauding clients and the market for years. Ben went from living in a mansion on the Upper East Side to a one-bed-roomed shack in Queens overnight.'

Shock and disbelief reverberated through Lia as she looked across the crowd again at that broad back. Of course she knew who Jonathan Carter was—his name was synonymous with the global financial crisis, and much of the blame had been apportioned to him.

Just then Ben turned around, and his blue gaze lasered straight onto her. She felt the pull all the way across the room.

From beside her, Ricardo said mournfully, 'What I wouldn't give for him to look at me like that.'

Lia forced a smile and made her way back across the room, feeling seriously confused after Ricardo's revelation. She thought back to when it had happened and figured that Ben must have been only in his early teens—if that.

When she got closer, she saw that a very glamorous woman beside Ben had a hand on his arm. She embodied dark-eyed sultry Brazilian sexiness, with generous curves that defied gravity. Immediately Lia felt a surge of something almost violent, and when Ben pulled her close to him with his free arm she found herself revelling in the proprietorial gesture.

The other woman's eyes flashed with displeasure, but she blasted Lia with a fake smile and walked away. Suddenly aware that she was acting very much out of character, Lia tried to pull away—but Ben wouldn't let her, turning so that she was pressed to his front.

'What are you doing?' She looked up at him. What Ricardo had told her was making her feel off-centre. He really had built himself up from nothing. After having had everything.

'I'm thinking that it's time to go home.'

Lia looked around, momentarily disorientated, and realised that the crowd had thinned out substantially. It was a lot later than she'd realised. She looked back to Ben, feeling hot when she noticed the growth of stubble on his jaw. He was so masculine. And there was so much more to him than she'd ever given him credit for. He wasn't the only one who was guilty of prejudice.

'Okay.' Her voice was husky. 'Let's go.'

He took her hand to lead her out, and as they said goodbye to their hosts Lia felt genuine emotion at the thought that she probably wouldn't meet them again. She'd enjoyed herself more than she'd expected. She'd had *fun*.

Once back in Ben's Jeep, she kicked off her sandals and stretched out her feet. She couldn't help sneaking glances at his profile, stern in the shadows of the car.

As they left the city behind them, Ben asked lightly, 'So, what were you and Ricardo talking about?'

Lia tensed, feeling guilty even though she knew it was irrational. She could have found out about his past if she'd dug a little deeper. Her own innate sense of honesty made her say, 'I didn't know that your father was Jonathan Carter.'

Ben's hand on the steering wheel tightened, his knuckles showing white. 'I should have guessed Ricardo wouldn't pass up the opportunity to gossip.'

Lia turned in her seat and rushed to defend the

man. 'It wasn't like that. I asked him how he knew you and he happened to mention—' She stopped, recalling the exact words. Maybe Ben's friend *had* been a little gossipy.

Ben said dryly, 'Do go on.'

Lia swallowed. 'He just mentioned that he thought it was amazing, all you'd achieved, considering how your family had lost everything.' When Ben didn't respond, Lia said, 'It's not exactly common knowledge.'

He glanced at her. 'You mean because it didn't come up when you did an internet search on me?'

She turned back to face the front and said hotly, 'That's hardly fair. You knew exactly who *I* was when you asked the matchmaker to set us up.'

Tension thickened in the intimate space of the car, and then Ben said with evident reluctance, 'The reason why my past doesn't always come up is because people choose to forget what's not relevant any more. It's old news.' His lips twisted. 'Especially after my father had the temerity to die in relative squalor and solitude with my mother following him a year later. I guess they figured he'd paid his dues.'

Sensing he wouldn't appreciate platitudes, Lia just asked, 'How did they die?'

'My father drank himself to death. He'd always been a heavy drinker—albeit of fine whiskies, when he could afford them. The cheaper stuff didn't suit his system so well. And my mother had a heart attack. She couldn't come to terms with what the real world looked like.'

Lia was silent, absorbing the enormity of what he'd just revealed. 'That's why you don't drink?'

He nodded, the lines of his face stern. Lia figured it was no surprise, after seeing his father poison himself. She knew enough about him now to know that he would consider that an immense failing in personal control.

She could imagine him as a young boy—handsome and privileged, no doubt attending the best schools, with his future mapped out. The world at his feet. Only to have it ripped apart and the grim reality of how things really were revealed. No wonder he'd thought he had her all summed up.

Sensing he'd appreciate a change in subject, she asked, 'So why Brazil? Do you have a special connection to here?'

Ben glanced at her again and she caught the

gleam of something wry in his expression. 'Did Ricardo stop gossiping long enough to answer your actual question?'

Lia frowned. 'He said that he'd seen some of your work in Manhattan...'

'Yes, and then he approached me with an offer to bid for the work on one of his hotels in Brazil. It was just when my company was starting to break even.'

'How old were you?' Lia asked.

Ben shrugged minutely. 'About twenty-five.'

Lia held in her shock. Some achievement, indeed. Clearly he'd been very driven, and questions abounded in her head as to what had happened after his mother had died. She knew what everyone else knew, about the foster homes, but how had he crawled out of that to achieve such meteoric success?

Ben continued. 'I went down to Bahia to see the site, and after a meeting Ricardo signed me up then and there. After completing the job I realised I'd come to love the place—it was like a breath of fresh air. Different, vibrant. Unstuffy. So I decided that I'd build a holiday home there. My family used to have a house in North Shore on Long Island. The community there, who had once been like family, completely ostracised us when my father lost everything. But as soon as I started to make a name for myself, some of my father's old cronies came out of the woodwork, as if nothing had happened. The last place I wanted to be was back in that stuffy environment.'

Lia could hear the bitterness in Ben's voice and read between the lines. Where had those 'friends' been when he'd been alone and defenceless?

Lia said lightly, 'Sounds like you made the right decision.'

She could feel him looking at her, but she didn't want him to see the mix of emotions she was try- ing to hide. She'd felt off-kilter from the moment she'd laid eyes on this man, and now it was even worse.

When Ben drove through the gates leading to his villa a short while later, Lia realised she'd been engrossed in her own circling thoughts. Ben got out of the driver's side and came around to help Lia out—the perfect gentleman. She only realised her feet were still bare when they hit the sharp gravel and she let out a squeak.

Before she knew what was happening she was

being lifted into Ben's arms and he was striding into the villa as if she weighed nothing.

'You don't have to carry me,' she said, but it was too late. They were inside, and he was putting her down.

Her head was whirling. She couldn't look at him, overwhelmed with some nameless emotion.

But Ben caught her chin with a finger and tipped her face up. He frowned. 'What is it?'

The fact that she felt absurdly close to tears was horrifying. She bit her lip, and then said, 'I don't know... I'm just...I'm sorry for what you went through. I can't imagine how awful it must have been.'

Ben's expression became shuttered in an instant, and he let her go so fast that she almost lurched forward.

He backed away, his lip curling. 'What? You're feeling sorry for me now because the poor little rich boy lost everything and had to slum it? Suddenly everything's more palatable now that you know I was born with a silver spoon in my mouth?'

Horror that he could think such a thing, and

hurt, made Lia put out a hand. '*No!* I didn't mean it like that at all—'

But he cut her off, saying harshly, 'It was the best thing that could have happened to me. It woke me up to reality before I could get too cushioned by life. I knew not to take anything for granted, as my father had done. Not to grow complacent. I learnt the value of hard work and building something with your own hands—something that won't collapse.'

'I can understand that,' Lia said quietly, hating it that he'd misunderstood her.

Ben looked at the woman in front of him, her hair tousled and that glorious dress falling to the floor where her bare feet peeped out. She was all slender curves and pale skin.

He knew he was wrong about her—that she wasn't a snob. And he knew what he'd just said hadn't been fair. But right now he was filled with something that was threatening to push him over the edge. He'd never revealed so much to anyone. Never spoken about his past like that. About his father's drinking. His mother's weakness.

Lia stepped forward, her hand out, her eyes wide and full of something Ben didn't want to decipher.

'Ben, I'm sorry, please let me explain—'

He tipped over that edge. *'No,'* he said harshly. 'You don't need to explain anything because I'm not interested in talking any more. All I'm interested in is *this...*'

Before she could say another word Ben had closed the distance between them, taken her face in his hands and was kissing her. Kissing her the way he'd been aching to kiss her again. For a long second she was frozen in his arms, and then she was moving closer and reaching up. Pressing her body against his.

Everything was forgotten as she twined her arms around his neck. Their angry words were decimated in the heat of this passion. Their mouths fused for a long moment, as if the intensity was too much to break, and then subtly Ben coaxed her to open her mouth to him. When his tongue touched hers he was lost, drowning in a sea of sensation and growing lust as he demanded a response, which she gave willingly.

He moved his hands down her back and settled them on her hips, hauling her closer. Close enough so she could feel what she was doing to him, where he ached most of all. Lia gasped into his mouth but he didn't let her break away. He never wanted to let her go again…

Between Lia's legs she felt damp and hot. Her breasts ached, pressed tight against his chest. But somehow a tiny sliver of sanity returned and she tore her mouth away from Ben's, breathing as if she'd just run a marathon.

They'd combusted. That was the only word for it. She'd never felt anything like it. She hadn't even known she was capable of this much feeling.

'I can't—' she gasped incoherently, too far gone to be embarrassed. 'This is too…too much.'

The look in Ben's eyes was hot and feral. 'It's not nearly enough.'

He caught her hand and led her deeper into the living room. Lia's body throbbed in time with the blood pumping to every erogenous zone. Ben took her over to one of the couches and made her sit down. She was glad, because her legs were shaking.

He stood above her, looking down with a kind

of intensity that scared and excited her in equal measure.

'You're so beautiful...'

She went to pull the edges of her dress together, feeling exposed, thinking of that buxom Brazilian beauty earlier. 'I'm not...'

He came down on his knees before her then, taking her by surprise. He put his hands on her thighs and gently pushed her legs apart, moving between them. His eyes burned into hers.

'Yes, you are. And I'm sorry for lashing out just now...you didn't deserve that.'

His apology struck at the heart of her. 'That's okay...'

He put his hands on her hips and pulled her towards him so that she lay back on the couch. She whispered through her erratic heartbeat. 'What are you doing?'

He smiled, but it was the smile of the devil. Dark and decadent. Sexy. 'Something I've wanted to do from the moment I saw you in this dress.'

He leant forward, putting delicious pressure on her between her legs, and slowly but methodically pushed her hands out of the way so that he could pull apart the neckline of her dress, all too easily.

Lia remembered his look in the shop, and instead of feeling self-conscious, something scarily exultant moved through her.

Her delicate underwired blue lace bra opened very conveniently from the front. Ben undid the catch and pushed the lace material aside. He cupped one full breast with his hand, making it pout upwards. Lia's breath stalled as shards of pleasure raced through her body. Excitement fizzed in her veins. And then Ben bent his head and tongued her nipple, bringing it to tingling hardness before he sucked it into his mouth.

Lia had a moment of sheer disbelief that this man could possibly want her this much before sensations she'd never felt before swamped her and removed her ability to think. Without even registering the movement, she found her hands were in Ben's hair and she was clutching him to her breast. Eyes shut, heart pounding…

He was reaching right down inside her and unlocking the door to all the insecurities she'd buried deep. And she couldn't stop him. Because the pleasure was eclipsing any fear she might be feeling—if she was even capable of being rational right now.

When Ben finally lifted his head from her tender flesh she opened her eyes, and it took her a second to focus and realise that she held his head in a death grip.

She let go immediately, horrified. But Ben just smiled. He lifted a hand and brushed some hair back off her cheek in a surprisingly tender move, even as she felt the hard length of his erection near the apex of her legs. She was aware that if she moved slightly it would create the friction she suddenly needed.

Who *was* she? What had she become?

'You look deliciously…undone.'

Ben's voice was gravelly. Lia looked at him, feeling twin desires: to move and pull her dress around her again, and also just to lie there and offer herself up to him.

He started to press kisses down her torso, his hands reaching around and finding where the dress was tied, undoing it easily, the silk like water in his hands. Soon he had her dress pushed apart completely, and he looked down at her blue lace panties.

Immediately Lia had a memory of her ex-fiancé, recoiling in horror when he'd first seen that she didn't shave all over, and she tried to sit up awkwardly, putting a hand down to cover herself.

Ben caught her, though, stopping her hand with his, looking at her. 'What is it?'

Now she felt horribly rational, and exposed and sane. Her ex-fiancé wasn't remotely in the same league as Ben, and if *he* had found that part of her a turn-off…

She looked away. 'I'm not…' She forced herself to look at him. 'I'm probably not like your usual lovers…'

Ben looked down between her legs and then back up, incredulous. 'Because you don't shave?'

Lia gulped. *God, this was excruciating.* She nodded. His face flushed and he took her hand and brought it down until he could place it over the bulge between his legs. The very hard bulge. Now she flushed.

'Sweetheart,' he growled, 'when I make love to a woman I like to know she's a woman. And right now I need to taste you, more than I've ever wanted to do anything else. Will you let me taste you?'

Something scarily exultant ripped through Lia. He wasn't turned off. He wanted to taste her. Did that mean he wanted to do what she'd seen Simon doing to his secretary when she'd walked in on them that day? The thought sent her mind reeling. It had looked so decadent to her at the time. And she'd never got over the jealousy that he'd been moved to do that to this lover, not to *her*... And now this man was asking her—

Before she could lose her nerve, Lia said huskily, 'Okay.'

Ben reached for the sides of her panties, expertly pulling them down and dropping them near her feet. She was bared completely now, the silk of the dress falling away as he pushed her thighs apart even more.

Lia closed her eyes and bit into her fist as Ben's head dropped and she felt his mouth on her soft inner thigh, pressing kisses and nipping at her skin gently. She was in danger of hyperventilating again, especially when his mouth moved higher, closer to the apex of her legs.

She didn't think he could spread her any wider but then he did, his big hands high on her thighs.

As if reading her mind, he commanded, 'Look at me.'

Reluctantly she opened her eyes. Ben had taken

off his shirt and his chest was bare and massive. She couldn't breathe as he bent forward and pressed his mouth to her, his tongue hot and wet as he dragged it up the secret folds of her body.

Lia's breath returned and she hitched in big gulps as that dark head bobbed and moved between her legs. His hands looked massive on her pale skin.

Ben looked up, 'Touch your breast.'

Feeling dizzy, even though she was all but lying down, Lia brought a hand to her breast, trapping a nipple between her fingers.

'Now, squeeze...' Ben instructed softly.

She did, and gasped as an arrow of pleasure went straight to her groin. Ben smiled and it was wicked as he bent his head again and tortured her with his mouth and tongue.

When he pushed a finger deep into the heart of her she arched her back off the couch, and then it became two fingers, thrusting in and out as his mouth and tongue lapped at her with fierce intensity.

Lia couldn't hold on. The coil of tension inside her snapped and she cried out as pleasure exploded her into tiny pieces. Waves of after-shocks rocked through her body for long moments, and she only became aware of her surroundings again when she could open her eyes and blink to focus, realising that Ben had lapped all that pleasure from her body and was now pressing lazy kisses to her inner thighs.

She felt undone. Turned inside out. Totally exposed but too spent to do anything about it. She realised that she was still squeezing her breast, almost painfully, and let go.

CHAPTER SIX

WHEN BEN FINALLY straightened up, tearing himself away from Lia's intoxicating taste and scent he was not prepared for the glorious sight of her looking so shocked. Her hair was a dark cloud around her head. The blue silk dress was crumpled beside those lush curves.

The realisation that she looked so stunned stopped him from automatically moving his hands to his belt to seek his own relief. He ignored the insistent ache in his pants and rested his hands on her knees. 'Are you okay?'

After a moment her eyes seemed to clear and she nodded. But he noticed that she reached for her dress with visibly shaking hands, pulling it over her as much as she could. The heat in Ben's blood cooled a little and he moved back so that she could pull her dress down, concealing that glorious body from view.

'What is it, Lia?'

She looked at him for a moment, almost accusingly, but he just looked right back. Making a little huffing sound, Lia scooted back on the couch until she was sitting upright. She bit her lip, but then eventually said, 'One day I walked into my ex-fiancé's office and found him with his secretary. He was doing what you just did to me to her...' She trailed off.

Ben tried to make sense of what she was saying. 'That's why you broke it off? He was unfaithful?'

She nodded jerkily, her face crimson now. 'Yes, but the thing is I've only ever slept with Simon...'

Ben would have never envisaged this scenario in a million years. In one fell swoop any remaining misconceptions he might have had about Julianna Ford were blasted apart. She was inexperienced, and she was achingly vulnerable right now, even though he could tell she hated it from the way her hands held her dress together in a white-knuckled grip.

And instead of feeling the urge to get up and run in the opposite direction Ben got up and sat on the couch beside her, feeling something close to protective.

Lia looked at him. 'I'm sorry. I'm not very experienced.'

Ben felt something dark rise up. 'What happened with this ex-fiancé?'

Now she went pale. 'When we made love for the first time…it hurt. A lot. After that I didn't really want to…to make love.' She grimaced. 'It wasn't as if we were in love. We'd both agreed to the marriage for our own reasons. But he told me that I was frigid, and that was why he was sleeping with his secretary. I couldn't…didn't want to get married after that.'

Ben reeled. He wanted to find that man and punch him for betraying this woman, for leaving her confidence in tatters. Never in Ben's life had he been remotely interested in the notion of taking a woman's virginity, but now he felt a ridiculous sense of loss, just imagining the way her rutting fiancé had probably not even realised the jewel he'd had in his hands. This woman was *not* frigid. Not remotely.

Then he thought of what else she'd just said. 'Why did you agree to a marriage of convenience?'

As if the questions were probing too deeply, Lia got up off the couch, still graceful even while she was deliciously dishevelled. She turned her back to Ben and pulled the dress around her, tying it in front.

When she turned around again it was all Ben could do not to yank her back down onto his lap.

She folded her arms over her chest, as if she could hear his lusty thoughts. 'It was primarily for my father. I told you…he's traditional. He believes I'll only be secure if I'm settled. He was sick a while back and I got a fright… He begged me to give Simon a chance—he knew he'd been asking me out on a regular basis.'

She shrugged and looked down, scuffing the floor with her toes. 'I went out with him and it turned out that we were both happy enough to agree to something more…clinical than a romantic relationship.' She looked back at Ben, almost defiant. 'At the time it seemed like a good idea.'

'You don't need to convince me,' Ben said with a bitter edge to his voice. 'After seeing how little there was to hold my parents' marriage together when the crisis hit, I'm under no illusions about the myth of a romantic ideal.'

For a long moment neither said anything else and then Lia took a step back.

Ben stood up. 'Where are you going?'

* * *

Middle Earth, hopefully.

Lia had been ready for the ground to open up and swallow her right from when she hadn't been able to stop the verbal equivalent of *This is My Life* from spilling out. She blamed Ben, and the fact that he'd wrung a response from her body that she'd never believed she'd feel.

He was looking at her now as if she had two heads, and the thought that he might pity her after what she'd just told him was making her burn with mortification. Of anything she might have expected from this man, she'd never expected that. Nor wanted it.

She struggled to look cool and calm, even though she was in tatters. 'I'm going to bed.'

Ben shook his head. 'We're not done here.'

Excitement and trepidation warred in Lia's chest. Ben was unmistakably alpha. Maybe he saw her as some kind of challenge?

'Look,' she said, 'I know this isn't what you expected when you thought of indulging in a weekend fling. I think we've established that I'm not exactly cast from the same mould as your usual women.'

She went to walk past him, instinctively seeking a place where she could be alone and deal with her sense of exposure without that incisive gaze watching her every move. He'd laid her bare—completely. She'd been right to resist him.

A hand on her arm stopped her. She looked up.

Ben pulled her around in front of him. 'There are no other women. There's only you. Are you saying you don't want this?'

Lia flushed at his words. *'There's only you.'* And how could she deny she wanted this when she'd just been writhing and moaning under his expert touch?

She said tightly, 'You really don't owe me anything, Ben. If you just feel sorry for—'

His hands tightened on her arms so much she stopped talking. He looked incredulous. 'Feel *sorry* for you? Believe me…that's the last thing I'm feeling right now. I want you, Lia. Because you make me feel like I'll combust if I don't have you. And that's not pity. That's desire.'

Suddenly she didn't have anything to hide behind. He was calling her out.

She felt nervous. 'I'm not experienced enough for you… I'll disappoint you.'

He speared her with that bright blue gaze, like two flames. 'You couldn't disappoint me if you tried, Lia. And there's no such thing as inexperience—there's just how two people fit together. You're not frigid—not remotely. That man was an idiot, and he couldn't recognise a brilliant precious gem when it was right in front of him.'

Ben's words reached deep inside her and melted the insecurity Lia had been carrying around like a weight.

He moved closer, as if sensing her vacillation. 'I want you, Lia, more than I've ever wanted another woman. But if you can say that you truly don't want this, then I'll let you go.'

He took her elbows in his hands and pulled her gently to him until they were touching. If she'd had any doubts about how much he wanted her, or thoughts that he just pitied her, they fled when she felt the hard, thrusting evidence of his desire against her soft belly.

Her heart started to pound and her blood heated. Her defences were annihilated. And then she felt a spike of anger. Anger that he'd brought her here and laid her bare, forced her to delve deep inside herself to where she ached and wanted…so much. Where she wanted *him*. Forcing her to admit it.

She felt fierce. 'I can't tell you that.'

Ben was intense. 'What can't you tell me?'

She looked up into his eyes and drowned. 'That I don't want you.'

Lia didn't care any more how or why she'd got here, just that she was, and she didn't want to be anywhere else. She desperately wanted Ben to show her again how she could respond to a man. That she wasn't frigid.

As if reading her mind, Ben bent and lifted her into his arms. And then he was carrying her up the stairs.

She was mesmerised by his jaw, by the play of the powerful muscles of his chest under her arm. Breathless at the thought of what she was doing, and so far out of her comfort zone that it wasn't funny, she pushed all her trepidation down.

Ben shouldered his way into his room, and Lia was vaguely aware that it was just as palatial as hers but more masculine in tones and colours. And then her gaze fell on the massive bed in the middle of the room and her mouth dried completely.

A part of her wanted to leap from Ben's arms and run away fast, but a stronger part realised that she wanted to be strong—for this, for herself. Her confidence had been eroded when she was a young child, when her own mother had rejected her, forcing her to shut away a part of herself for fear of rejection. Then she'd let Simon decimate her confidence as a sexual woman. It was time to restore the balance.

Ben put her down near the bottom of the bed. His voice was deep, rumbling in the silence. 'You can let your dress go.'

Lia looked down and saw her almost white-knuckled grip on her dress. She uncurled her fingers, undid the tie and let it go. It swung open, catching on the slopes of her breasts.

She heard a sharp intake of breath and looked up to see Ben's eyes on her.

'So beautiful,' he muttered as he brought his hands to her shoulders and pulled her dress off them and down over her arms, until it fell to the floor in a sibilant *whoosh* of silk. Her undone bra followed.

Now she was naked, the ends of her hair tickling the bare skin of her shoulders. Ben's eyes had darkened and Lia gritted her jaw to kill the instinct to cover herself with her arms; she didn't want him to see how vulnerable she really felt. No doubt he was used to women parading themselves in front of him.

Instead, just to do something to break the almost overwhelming tension, she reached out and touched his chest tentatively. It was muscled perfection, broad and strong. Defined pectorals with a dusting of dark curling hair led down to the ridges of a six-pack and his flat belly, with its single line of dark hair dissecting the muscles and disappearing under his trousers.

Ben sucked in a breath and, emboldened, Lia explored further, spreading her hands across his chest. They looked tiny and pale next to that burnished skin. She could feel his heart thumping solidly, and some nameless emotion gripped her tight. But she ignored it. Now was not the time for emotion.

She raked her nails over him experimentally, catching a nipple, making him take another sharp intake of breath. He caught the back of her head, his fingers tangling in her hair. She looked up and felt drugged.

Not taking her gaze off his, she let her hands feel their way to his lean waist and found where his belt was buckled. She looked down and undid it, and then her hands were on his button and the zip. She could feel the insistent thrust of his erection through his clothes, and a wave of heat scorched her from the inside out and between her legs, where she felt damp again. Hot.

She pushed his trousers down over his hips and he stepped out of them, letting her go momentarily. Then he pulled down his briefs until he too was gloriously naked. She'd never been more aware of herself as a woman. There was something very elemental about this moment, with everything stripped away.

Unable to resist, and not even recognising herself any more, Lia reached out and encircled his hard flesh with her hand, stroking him up and down, mesmerised by the vulnerability of his erection and also the steely strength. The velvet texture of his skin. She touched the bead of moisture at its head and spread it with her thumb.

At that Ben took her hand from him and she looked up.

'I won't last if you keep touching me like that.'

He caught her hand and brought her around the side of the bed, urged her down onto it, following her. He looked massive from where she lay, all wide shoulders and chest and long, lean body.

Every nerve in her body was tingling. She could feel Ben's erection against her thigh, hard and heavy. *Big.* She felt a shiver of trepidation, remembering the discomfort she'd felt with her fiancé and how she'd failed to excite him, but again, as if reading her mind, Ben distracted her by moving between her legs, spreading them wide.

With his elbows trapping her, he cupped both her breasts and teased her tingling nipples with his thumbs, before lowering his head and sucking first one and then the other into his hot mouth, torturing her with his wicked tongue.

As the flames of lust licked higher and higher Lia moaned softly. She wanted to squirm, to arch her back, but her movements were restricted by Ben's big body holding hers down. It was an exquisite form of torture, and as he lavished attention on her breasts he moved subtly against her, notching his hips higher, until she could feel the blunt head of his erection move against her where she was slick with desire.

She widened her legs even more and tried to move her hips up, wanting him to fill the part of her that ached. Then she heard a muttered curse and Ben suddenly rolled away.

Lia lifted her head. She realised she was panting. 'What's wrong?'

For an awful second she went cold, imagining that he'd realised she wasn't enough for him… But then she saw him extract something from a drawer beside the bed, heard foil tear, and then he was rolling protection onto his thick length.

Relief flooded her and she lay back. Ben knelt between her legs. Lia was all but splayed before him, like some kind of offering. But then, instead of coming over her again as she'd expected—*as she wanted*—he reached out a hand and touched her where she ached most. Where she was embarrassingly wet for him.

He circled her with his thumb, ratcheting up the tension inside her. Dipping inside, and out again, lubricating her with her own juices.

'You want me.'

She wondered how on earth he could doubt it.

Then she gasped and her back arched as he slid two fingers into her. She said jerkily, 'I told you I did.'

Lia could feel her muscles tighten around his fingers. Heard him curse softly. She felt too exposed. She didn't want him to make her come like this, while he watched.

She reached out and wrapped her hands around his arms. 'Please... Ben, I need...' Her back arched again as he thrust his fingers deeper, playing her like a violin. She lifted her head, hating the power he had over her right now, and said fiercely, 'I need *you*.'

Ben finally took his hand away, and then he loomed over her, his thighs pushing hers apart, and she slid her hands up to his shoulders.

'Look at me,' he said roughly. 'Don't *ever* doubt that you are a very desirable woman, Lia.'

She looked down and saw him take himself in his hand as he guided himself towards her, and then he fed himself into her body, slowly, inch by inch, making her draw her breath in on one long inhale as he impaled her...*utterly.*

He was big...bringing her almost to the edge of discomfort. But he held himself still for a long moment, letting her body adjust to him. And then, when she took another breath, he started to move, and everything in Lia's world was reduced to the here and now. This moment. This man. And the exquisite sensations rushing through her body.

She'd never felt anything like it as a wholly new tension built inside her with every movement of Ben's body in and out of hers. She wrapped her legs around his back, heels digging into his taut muscles. His hand gripped her thigh and his movements became less careful, a little rougher.

He came closer, moved down over her, making his chest hair abrade her still sensitive nipples. She reached up and found his mouth, and as everything inside her coiled to a point of excruciating pleasure/pain she pressed a desperate kiss to his mouth until finally she was broken apart into a million shattering pieces.

She was barely aware of Ben's own shout as his body tensed over hers for a long moment, muscles locked and taut as a paroxysm of pleasure held him in its grip too.

When Lia woke she felt completely disorientated, recognising that she wasn't in her own bed, or room. And then she felt the unfamiliar aches in her body and memory came rushing back.

Dawn was breaking outside, bathing Ben's room in a pink pearlescent hue that didn't diminish the masculine tones one bit. Gingerly, Lia moved her head, and sucked in a breath when she saw the unashamedly male and indolent sprawl of a very naked Benjamin Carter beside her.

Even like this, in repose, he was magnificent... Dark stubble lined his jaw, making him look rakish. Long lashes should have prettified the stark and strong lines of his face but they didn't. He looked marginally less fierce, especially when those blue eyes weren't watching her and gauging her reaction to every little thing. She might hate him for that if she wasn't feeling so...*sated.*

Her gaze travelled down over hard muscles and her face grew hot when she saw that most masculine and potent part of him—no less impressive at rest.

They'd made love again last night, after that first cataclysmic time. The second time had been slower, more luxurious, but no less intense. A surge of emotion made her throat tight. She wasn't frigid. *At all.* In fact the woman revealed under

Ben's expert tutelage was sensual and voracious...
and he had shown her that. As easily as flicking
a switch to let light into a dark room.

Lia sucked in a breath. That was exactly what
he'd done. He'd shone light into the dark corners
of her soul, where she'd felt closed-off. Deficient.

His expert dismantling of her defences had started
yesterday. By the time they'd gone to his friends'
party they'd already been crumbling, thanks to
their idyllic day spent walking around one of the
most beautiful cities in the world, with surely one
of its most charismatic and charming guides...

A voice mocked her: who was she kidding? Her
defences had been crumbling from the moment
she'd bumped into him outside the Algonquin
Hotel in New York.

And then something cold flickered down Lia's
spine as she registered the full magnitude of just
how easily and completely she'd capitulated. It
really hadn't taken much at all, in the end. She'd
proved no less susceptible than any other woman
to this man. Finding out about his troubled past
had only added another layer of depth to a man
who was fast becoming far too complex and fas-
cinating.

And now there was this—the ultimate intimate exposure. She'd slept with him because he'd made love to her mind as much as to her body. He'd delved deep and she'd let him in, far more than anyone else.

Emotions she'd never felt before rushed around her in a sickening mix...fear, exultation, hope.

It was the hope that brought her back to earth with a bang. Hope...for *what*? The kind of thing she'd always told herself didn't exist? Hope that she wouldn't face the excruciating lash of rejection if she opened herself up to someone?

As Ben had said himself the previous evening: *'I'm under no illusions about the myth of a romantic ideal.'* And neither was she, she assured herself, but for a dizzying moment there she'd felt hope—and that was dangerous.

The thought of Ben waking, and of herself trying to act blasé when she had no idea how to navigate this kind of situation, made her go cold all over. She had nowhere left to hide.

Her mother's abandonment had not only devastated her father—it had devastated Lia. The knowledge that she hadn't been lovable enough to make her stay had been indelibly inked into her skin from a young age, and Lia knew now that that was at the heart of why she'd avoided intimacy for so long, and why she'd agreed to a marriage of convenience.

She'd found it easy to dissociate, not to engage, because no one had ever broken down the walls she'd erected…until now. The galling reality that she could be as susceptible to heartbreak as her father after years of avoiding it made her feel nauseous.

Ben would see through her in an instant—see all her weaknesses. And, worse, possibly even see that flicker of hope. The part of her that wasn't half as cool and collected as she'd always thought she was. Impervious to fickle emotions.

Lia slid out of the bed, making not a sound. Ben moved minutely, frowning in his sleep, but then he relaxed again, and her heart pounded with a mixture of panic and desperation.

Benjamin Carter had somehow managed to slide under her skin enough to make her realise that all the foundations she'd worked so hard to build up were far shakier than she liked to admit. And that was enough to drive Lia as far away from this man as she could go.

* * *

The following morning Ben padded through the villa in a pair of hastily pulled on shorts with an uncomfortable feeling of foreboding prickling along his skin. He'd woken shortly before to find the space beside him in bed empty. And Lia hadn't been in the bathroom.

When he'd woken, at first he'd registered a deeper feeling of satisfaction than he'd ever felt before. A memory had surfaced: after they'd made love again last night Lia had been draped over his body, her head in the crook between his head and neck, her body a deliciously curved and pliant weight on his.

He'd stroked his hand up and down her back and said gruffly, 'See? I told you… It's nothing to do with experience. We *fit*.'

She'd made a huffing noise into his skin, clearly too exhausted to speak. And Ben had smiled… before falling asleep and waking to find her gone.

Ben didn't usually wake with the expectation of finding a woman in his bed—he preferred to keep that boundary firmly intact—but it hadn't even entered his head with Lia.

He frowned now, when he saw she wasn't in

the main living area, but still wasn't unduly concerned. She had to be here somewhere.

For the first time in days, since he'd first laid eyes on her, Ben's head was feeling clear again. He'd known he wanted her, but he hadn't expected their chemistry to be so explosive. And when he found her he was going to convince her to stay another day... He was going to woo her and persuade her to consider marriage—because if she'd considered it once before she'd have to be open to the option again—in spite of the way it had turned out. Clearly it meant a lot to her father, and he obviously meant a lot to her.

Lia Ford was not the one-dimensional person he had believed her to be at the very start. She was bright, sharp, compassionate, *passionate*.

He thought about how he'd felt claustrophobic when the idea of taking a wife had first been mentioned to him...how he'd felt when he'd sat down to discuss it with the Sheikh and the others. But now the prospect of making Lia Ford his wife appealed to Ben in a way that he hadn't ever thought it would.

He realised that he'd seriously underestimated how much a woman like Lia could contribute to his life. They had ideals and goals in common. The more he thought about it, the less he felt inclined to take a wife who would just be meek and biddable. He wanted someone with fire, and Lia had that in spades. She was spirited and unafraid to stand up to him, and he liked that.

And for the first time he even found himself thinking of children. Of what it would be like to have a son or a daughter. Something in Ben's chest grew tight at the thought of a small dark-haired child with sparkling blue eyes running around.

He'd never allowed himself to contemplate it before, because his own experience of watching his parents crumble so catastrophically under the strain of their lives self-destructing had scarred him enough to never want to risk subjecting any child of his to that.

But now he felt he could consider it for the first time. A woman like Lia would never crumble. She would get up and start again. Their marriage would be nothing like his parents'—falling apart like a flimsy structure at the first inkling of trouble.

Ben was in the kitchen now, but that too was empty. He ignored his growing unease and the fact that the villa was too quiet. As much as he admired Lia's independence, and the fact that she obviously wasn't one of those women who liked to cling like an octopus the morning after, he just wanted to find her now.

A sense of relief hit him when he thought of the beach—of course she'd be there. But when he walked out onto the pristine sand, he saw that his stretch of private beach was empty. No supple pale body was lying out under an umbrella.

He heard a sound and whirled around, but it was just Esmé, carrying flowers into the villa. She called out sunnily, 'Morning, Boss. You slept late—not like you at all.'

Ben felt like scowling at the reminder that last night had made its mark, but he forced a smile, following Esmé back into the villa. 'Have you seen Lia?'

She whirled around, frowning. 'You don't know?'

Ben was seriously struggling to hold his irritation in. 'Know what?'

Esmé put the exotic blooms carefully on a table, her face a picture of quizzical innocence. 'She left early this morning. When Joao dropped me off, she got a lift with him back into Salvador. She said she had to take the first flight to New York today, then get back to the UK. I presumed you knew… She said she didn't want to wake you and left you a note. I put it in your office.'

As Ben watched Esmé start to put the blooms in a large vase on the table in the centre of the hall he felt something wide and uncomfortable open up in his chest. And sheer incomprehension. No woman *ever* walked away from him. But this one had. Twice now.

He turned before Esmé could make anything of his reaction, went to his office and saw the folded-over note with *'Ben'* written on it in a very feminine script. He opened it to read.

Dear Ben,
Thank you again for your kind donation to the charity. I think after last night the terms of the bid are well and truly fulfilled. After all, this was never going to go beyond the week-end, was it?
I've enjoyed my time here in Bahia—thank you. I doubt I'll run into you again.
Best wishes,
Lia Ford.

The chasm opening up in Ben's chest snapped shut suddenly and became a hard, heavy weight. The insinuation that she'd slept with him more to fulfil the terms of the bid and less because she'd wanted to was not welcome.

He crushed the piece of paper in his hands as something broke the heavy weight apart—anger.

He'd underestimated her—*again*. But she'd underestimated him if she thought that she wouldn't run into him again. He was going to make very sure that she did run into him again—and this time she would not be running away. Because she was perfect for him. And no way was he letting her, or this opportunity, slip out of his grasp.

CHAPTER SEVEN

'WHERE'S YOUR FATHER, LIA? Not ill again, I hope?'

Lia felt like hitting the smug smile off the face of one of her father's biggest competitors, who was making it very obvious that he *did* hope her father was ill, but instead she smiled beatifically and said, 'Of course he's not ill, George.' Her smile stayed fixed as she went on, 'He's actually too busy to be here this evening—which is why I have to say I'm surprised to see *you* here. Didn't you know that this evening is the construction union's annual winter party?'

The man's already florid face grew redder as he blustered, 'Well, yes, of course I did…but I wouldn't normally think of going to one of those events—'

Which is why you're only a fraction as successful as my father, she thought to herself privately, even as she said a placatory, 'No, of course not. Most people don't. He will insist on going, though—every year—and his employees seem to love him for it.'

The man was backpedalling away from Lia so fast that she nearly laughed out loud. It was a little mean of her, she knew, to tease him like that. But in fairness her father *had* put in an appearance at the union party largely because it wouldn't be filled with vultures ready to pick him apart to see just how robust he was.

She'd just been informed that he was back, via one of his usual slightly ham-fisted texts, which was all in caps.

I'M HOME NOW. DON'T WORRY. HOLD THE FORT FOR ME, DARLING. DAD. XX

Lia sighed. That was what she felt as if she'd been doing all her life. Holding the fort for her father, who had never really recovered after her mother's abandonment of them both. But she pushed that moment of uncharacteristic self-pity out of her mind now. She didn't want anyone here at this exclusive London charity bash to suspect for a second that everything wasn't absolutely fine.

So she pasted on another bright smile when she saw two more of her father's biggest rivals bearing down on her, with glints in their eyes. But just before they reached her something in her peripheral vision made her look to her left and her heart stopped beating. Almost literally stopped.

It was Benjamin Carter, standing at the main doorway, dressed in a classic black tuxedo, scanning the room as if looking for something. Or some*one*. His bright blue gaze—visible even from where she stood—landed on her and stopped. Lia felt its impact immediately, deep in her body, like an electrical shock.

Everything dropped away. She was aware of voices from nearby, aware that she was meant to be responding to something, but had no idea to what.

It felt as if seconds had passed since she'd seen him, but it had actually been a week.

A week since she'd left this man lying on his bed amongst tangled sheets, with her heart pounding so hard she'd been able to feel it. It started again now, as he walked towards her, and she drank him in helplessly. He looked taller, darker, and more handsome against the backdrop of this much paler British crowd.

For an awful second she wondered if she was

hallucinating—she'd believed she'd never see him again, and had done her best all week to repress the memories and images. But at night her subconscious hadn't been able to stem the tide, and each morning she'd woken hot and sweaty, with the sheets tangled around her body after X-rated dreams.

He closed the distance between them with long strides, the crowd parting like water and hushed whispers following his progress. He reached Lia and she was struck mute.

Without taking his eyes off hers, he said, 'Gentlemen, please excuse the interruption, but I have some unfinished business with Miss Ford.'

And then he reached for Lia's hand, taking it in a firm grip, and started walking back out of the room, taking her with him. The lust that flooded her body at the touch of his hand told her that she wasn't hallucinating—as did the excitement mixed with shock in her blood.

Lia had to lift her long black silk dress in one hand, afraid of tripping. She caught sight of herself and Ben in a long mirror and saw that she looked tiny behind him, her shoulders bare in the long strapless dress, her hair upswept into a rough chignon.

Panic flooded her system as the reality sank in that he was really here. If he guessed for a second how deep he'd sneaked under her skin… The panic intensified. She dug her heels in and tried to pull her hand free, but his only tightened.

He stopped and turned around, a fierce expression on his face. Gone was the civil, suave man she'd first met. He was angry. But instead of feeling intimidated she found her anger matched his. Anger at him for coming into her world like this. For upsetting her equilibrium again.

'What the hell do you think you're doing?' she snapped. 'You're on my turf now.'

Ben arched a brow. 'Oh, forgive me, Lady Ford, do you own this hotel?'

She flushed. 'No, of course not.' Then she arched her own brow. 'Do you have a private plane stashed on the lawn at the back? Are you planning another little kidnap stunt?'

He kept her hand firmly in his and faced her fully, his free arm snaking around her waist and pulling her close. She went on fire when she felt his burgeoning erection between them. His eyes gleamed when he saw her reaction. Lia was acutely aware of the audience around them, and cursed herself for not waiting to confront him until they were somewhere more private.

'You asked me a question.'

Lia frowned. 'What question?'

'In that kind note you left, you said—and I quote—*"This was never going to go beyond the weekend, was it?"*'

Lia flushed hotter. 'That was a rhetorical question.'

Ben shook his head. 'Not any more—because I believe I've just answered it.'

'How?'

He moved against her subtly, explicitly, leaving her in no doubt as to what he meant. Then he said throatily, 'I suggest you come with me right now—unless you want to treat your peers to the kind of show they'd prefer to watch in private or on pay per view.'

Some emotion Lia didn't want to name surged through her as the knowledge sank in—*she wasn't dreaming.* He was here and he still wanted her. And, heaven help her, she wanted him too… She'd run scared in Brazil, but right now she couldn't exactly recall why it had been so imperative to get away from him.

Displaying his uncanny ability to read her mind, Ben was making the most of her hesitation and continuing on his journey out of the room, leading her into the hushed lobby of the very exclusive London hotel.

A lift door opened nearby and Ben diverted suddenly, pulling her in with him just as the doors closed again, almost catching Lia's dress. The lift started to ascend. And suddenly in the confined space, with Ben taking up most of the room with his big body, the panic returned. He really was here. And now she really had nowhere to hide.

'This is crazy, Ben! You can't just remove me to wherever you like, whenever you like.'

She watched as he hit a button with the palm of his hand and the lift shuddered to a halt. Between floors. He finally let her hand go, and caged her in with a hand on either side of her head.

'I have issues with your note,' he said, in a low, deep drawl that impacted Lia right between her legs.

The panic was draining away, to be replaced by something hot and illicit in her blood. And, more dangerously, the memories she'd been re-pressing all week were starting to break free of their moorings, flooding her brain with images and rising desire.

'Primarily,' he continued, oblivious to her inner turmoil, 'the bit where you assumed that our… liaison wouldn't last beyond the weekend.'

Lia was feeling breathless. Was it her imagina-tion or were the mirrors in the elevator starting to steam up? She struggled to recall what he'd just said, and then asked, 'Is that what it was? A liaison?'

Again, as if she hadn't spoken, Ben said, 'Do you really think I spent all that money just to get you into my bed?'

Lia wanted to squirm. Of course she didn't. Not any more. But that was where the danger lay…in thinking about what he wanted from her outside of this insane heat. Or, worse, what *she* wanted. When she'd protected herself for so long—even going so far as to agree to a marriage of conve-nience.

She shook her head now. 'No, I don't think that.'

A slow, sexy grin spread across Ben's face and Lia's legs immediately felt weak. The tension thickened between them. He wasn't going anywhere.

The giddy recklessness she'd felt in New York came back. Maybe he was here to finish what they'd started in Brazil. One more night? Two? And then he'd go back to his own life. After all, she reminded herself through the gathering heat in her brain, Ben didn't *do* relationships, did he?

And neither did she. She shouldn't have panicked in Brazil—it could have burnt out there. But she had. And now he was here. So maybe it would be okay to just…let it burn out. Here, as opposed to there. Did the geographics matter?

The fevered circling thoughts all led to one conclusion: Lia giving herself permission to stop fighting the inevitable. Resistance melted and she dived into the fever growing in her blood.

'Kiss me, Ben.'

Stop the chatter in my head, a small voice begged.

He smiled, wickedly accepting her capitulation—*again*—and then he cupped her face in his hands, tilted it up to his, and kissed her, stroking his tongue into her mouth, deep. Reminding her of the exquisite pleasure he'd given her, and the gift of the knowledge that she wasn't cold inside.

That alone made emotion surge again, and Lia wrapped her arms tight around his neck as if that would contain it. He'd flown all the way across the world to kiss her like this, deep and hot and wicked. And she would take it—because this was finite.

She arched her body into his, her blood throbbing in time with her heart when she felt the very masculine evidence of his arousal against her. His hands moved down her sides to her buttocks, where he cupped her through the slippery material of the dress.

He pulled back long enough to speak as he lifted her up, instructing, 'Wrap your legs around my hips.'

She did it mindlessly, her dress sliding high on her thighs as he lifted her effortlessly. She hooked her legs around his waist. Kissing her again, Ben slipped a hand underneath the dress and explored between the lace of her panties and her bottom, caressing her bare skin. She moaned into his mouth, dizzy.

Her bare upper back was against one mirrored wall of the lift, and Ben angled his hips so that the bulge of his erection pressed against her, between her legs, where she was wet and hot.

Her dress felt too tight. But even as she was thinking that Ben was sliding his fingers under the top of it and pulling it down, so that one of her breasts was freed. He pulled back from the kiss, and stared at her. He looked drunk, dazed.

Lia was vaguely aware that the only things holding her up were the wall and Ben's hand on her bottom. Because now he was thumbing her nipple and she was biting her lip.

'Please...' she begged.

He looked at her, and some hair flopped forward onto his forehead.

She brushed it back, feeling inordinately tender. 'Touch me...like you did before.'

He smiled, and it was wicked. He lowered his head and flicked his tongue against her straining nipple. He looked back up, all innocence. 'Like this?'

'Yes...' Lia growled, feeling even needier now. 'Damn you...*more.*'

His eyes flashed and he lowered his head to her breast and took her nipple deep into his mouth. Lia tensed, to try and hold off falling over the edge, but Ben was remorseless and his hips were making thrusting movements against her… All he'd have to do would be to slide her panties aside and free himself and he'd be inside her, where she needed him so badly.

Shocked at the completely wanton direction of her thoughts, and at how desperate her desire was, Lia's eyes snapped open.

In the reflection of the mirror behind Ben she saw her long pale legs, wrapped around his slim hips, and his dark head at her breast. She saw her own flushed face, blue eyes glittering fiercely. Her hair was mussed and her mouth was swollen. And they were in a lift.

She tensed even more and gripped Ben's hair, pulling his head up. 'We can't make love here—in a lift.'

Ben looked about ready to refute that statement, but then he seemed to come to his senses and straightened up, removing the delicious friction of his body from Lia's. She immediately felt bereft.

'Actually,' she said, feeling reckless and changing her mind abruptly, 'I've never made love in a lift…the idea is growing on me.'

Ben looked stubborn. 'No way. You're right.

I'm not going to be the crass American caught *in flagrante delicto* in one of London's most exclusive hotels.'

Lia felt a little shard pierce her. He was not crass—at all. Ben unhooked her legs from his hips and helped her stand again. She was wobbly on her feet and only belatedly realised her breast was still exposed when the lift started moving again. Ben efficiently covered her up, his fingers brushing against her sensitive skin.

Just in time, too, because the doors opened and an older couple with severe expressions got in, muttering about how long they'd had to wait for the lift. Lia had to stifle her giggles and Ben took her hand, gripping it tight.

The lift came to a halt again and she followed him out, not having a clue where they were going until he stopped outside a door and unlocked it with a hotel key. The fact that he'd booked a room at the hotel made something bloom in her chest— something she hadn't allowed room to breathe since she'd taken that flight from Salvador, back to New York and then home.

Hope.

The door shut behind them and Ben had her

lifted against it with her legs around his hips before she could take another breath.

'Now,' he said throatily, 'where were we?'

Dawn was breaking outside when Lia awoke. For
a few seconds she lay there, blinking, taking stock
of all the pleasurable aches in her body. She was
aware that her dress was hanging precariously
off the end of the bed, and that there was a trail
of destruction along the floor from the doorway
to the bed, of her underwear.

She blushed when she thought of the urgency of
their lovemaking against the door of the suite...
and then the much more languid second time...
and the third.

She turned her head to see Ben sprawled in unashamedly masculine splendour. Déjà vu made
her feel momentarily dizzy and her heart hitched.
Instinctively she started to move, but those blue
eyes snapped open and before she could take another breath he had her trapped under one powerful thigh, a hand on her breast. Lia's blood leapt,
and her sleepy body was awake and humming in
seconds.

'Where do you think you're going?'

His voice was deliciously rough. Lia could feel

her nipple peaking under his palm and he moved it so that he could flick it with his thumb, rousing it to a sharp point. She almost groaned, but forced herself to put her hand over his—which didn't really help.

All her bravado, and the justifications she'd used in order to acquiesce to Ben's lovemaking last night, felt flimsy in the cold morning light. Her emotions were too raw all of a sudden.

'I should go.'

Ben ignored her hand on his and continued torturing her breast. He also subtly moved his thigh, so that his erection nestled close to the juncture of Lia's legs.

'I think that's a very bad idea.'

Ben bent his head and started to press kisses along the exposed shoulder nearest to him. His hand deftly dislodged hers and he pinched her nipple between his fingers, just as his hot mouth found and started torturing her other breast.

Not able to hold back the groan this time, Lia felt all resistance fade as Ben's hand smoothed its way down over her belly to between her legs, pushing them apart so his questing fingers could seek and discover for himself how much she wanted him—again. Already.

He lifted his head and smiled smugly. A surge of irritation at her own weakness galvanised Lia to move and she took him by surprise, coming up to straddle him, her hands holding his arms back behind his head. She knew he could break free easily, but it was still momentarily heady to have him at her mercy, however illusory.

She moved her body back until she could feel the head of his erection against her and, keeping it between them, slowly started to move up and down, sliding her body along his thick length, seeing his face flush and his pupils dilate.

'Witch,' he ground out, and she could feel him lengthen and grow harder under her.

Their breathing became more laboured as Lia obeyed the dictates of her body to go faster, press down harder. Ben lifted his head and captured her nipple, biting gently with his teeth. It sent a shudder all the way down to between Lia's legs.

And then, proving how little control she really wielded over him, Ben moved and she was flat on her back, trapped under him again. He reached for protection and expertly rolled it over his erection, and then, before Lia could take another breath, he was sinking deep inside her, his eyes on hers, not letting her escape for a moment.

The climax that broke over them came swiftly and was brutal in its power, washing everything else away. And in the shuddering aftermath, when Ben pulled Lia close and wrapped his arms and legs around her, something inside her just… melted.

Lia was feeling marginally restored as she belted a thick robe around herself after taking a quick shower. When she'd woken again Ben hadn't been in the bed and she'd spied him in the living area, dressed in dark trousers and a long-sleeved thin grey jumper that did nothing to disguise his muscles. He was pacing up and down while talking on his mobile phone, so she'd taken quick advantage, locking herself in the bathroom.

She'd avoided looking at herself in the mirror, not wanting to see the aftermath of their cataclysmic night and morning. She'd also avoided letting her mind stray to dangerous thoughts like, *Why did he come here really?* And, *What happens now?* She'd decided she was just going to nip it in the bud now because sleeping with Ben again had only reinforced her fears about not being as emotionally detached as she'd like to be. As he undoubtedly was.

When she padded into the living area of the plush suite, Ben was seated at the table, reading a newspaper. He put it down as she approached and that blue gaze swept her up and down. Even under the thick robe she could feel herself respond.

'I've ordered some clothes for you to change into.'

For a second she felt inordinately touched at his consideration *and* relief for the fact that she wouldn't have to do the walk of shame out of the hotel, into the glaring London daylight. 'Thanks, I'll pay you back.'

His eyes flashed at that, but he let it go as she sat down and looked at the array of breakfast/ brunch items laid out. 'I wasn't sure what you'd like, so I ordered a selection.'

Lia slid into a chair, avoiding his eye. Her pitifully few experiences of morning-after situations with her ex-fiancé had been sterile, dispassionate affairs—she'd never experienced this intense level of awareness before.

'Coffee will do for now.'

Ben reached for a tall slender pot and poured fragrant coffee into a cup. She couldn't take her eyes off his hands: large and masculine, yet elegant, too. She fought back a blush as she thought of how they'd felt on her skin, and took a quick sip of coffee to try and dislodge her lurid memories.

When she felt able, she looked at him. 'So… what's your plan while you're here in London?'

Ben looked at her and a small smile played around his sensual mouth. '*You*, Lia. You're my plan.'

To hear him confirm that he really was here just because of her was seriously disarming—and overwhelming. Emotion swelled and it made her want to push him back.

She put down her cup with a jarring clatter of porcelain. 'You can't expect me just to drop everything to accommodate you. I have a life here… work.'

Ben's eyes narrowed on her. 'Work for your father? Like you were doing last night…being his emissary?'

Lia felt immediately defensive. 'It's a family business.'

'But what about your plans for your own work?'

She immediately regretted telling him all that she had. 'I don't think you're here to discuss my career options.'

Ben inclined his head slightly in concession. 'Not really, no. But as it happens I have an office here in London. I'm taking advantage of the trip to check in with my team on the ground. We've got several projects in development, and they're setting up some meetings for me while I'm here.'

Lia cursed herself for not guessing that he had an office in London, or checking.

He leaned forward then. 'But, more importantly, I want to get to know you better, Lia. That's really why I'm here.'

Her silly heart hitched as trepidation warred with that illicit sense of hope. She'd run from this in Bahia and he'd chased her down. She was afraid that she wasn't strong enough to walk away again. And he knew it.

Ben felt a surge of triumph when Lia didn't immediately jump up from the table at his declaration that he wanted to spend time with her, and tried to hide it from his expression.

Even though she'd acquiesced to him last night, he'd known she'd be prickly in the morning—no doubt lambasting herself for her weakness. And he knew that a large part of why she'd succumbed had been because he'd all but ambushed her.

He was still reeling from the effects of seeing her again after a week. He had intended to come to London, find Lia at the charity function where he knew she'd be, and woo her. Show her how determined he was to get to know her. But he'd taken one look at her across that crowded room and something inside him had turned feral. He'd *had* to have her. And then he'd morphed into some kind of caveman, all but dragging her into that lift, and if she hadn't stopped them when she had…

But he could see now that her expression was closing off, becoming shuttered. Those beautiful eyes becoming unreadable.

He shook his head, 'Don't do that, Lia.'

She looked slightly alarmed. 'Do what?'

'Retreat behind that prim wall you put up.'

He reached for her, taking her hand and pulling her out of her seat and over to him before she could object. He tugged her down into his lap and stifled a groan when she came into contact with a still sensitive part of his anatomy. The hunger he felt for her was alarming…he was used to it diminishing with a lover. But what he felt for Lia was getting stronger.

Ben knew that if he hadn't been there because he wanted to woo her into considering a very long-term arrangement with him, then he would most likely be running from the intensity he felt when he was around her.

He assured himself that it was all part of the plan. Lia was important to him because of what she represented. The fact that they were combustible in bed was a bonus he had every intention of exploiting to its full potential.

She looked at him, with a wary expression on her face that made Ben wonder if she was reading his mind.

'What are we doing here, Ben?'

If any other woman had asked him that question Ben would definitely be running. But right now the last thing he felt was an urge to leave.

'Well, for a start, we're not leaving this hotel room for the whole weekend.' He could see Lia's immediate reaction to that—rejection—and he said quickly, 'Look, neither of us is what the other expected—would you agree?'

Slowly, she nodded her head. 'I guess so.'

Ben started moving his hand in small circles on her back. His other hand was on her thigh and he exerted slight pressure, seeing how her eyes flared with heat. He would use everything in his arsenal if he had to—unashamedly.

'I want to know more about you. And there's too much heat between us to walk away yet. Spend the weekend with me.' Ben mentally assured himself that by the end of the weekend Lia would be his—in more ways than one. Didn't women find whirlwind affairs romantic?

His hand explored underneath her robe to find the silky skin of her bare thigh. He felt the immediate reaction of her body.

She put her hands on his chest. When she spoke again, her voice was breathy. 'Look, I—'

She stopped and bit her lip when Ben's hand delved between her thighs, opening them slightly. She tried to glare at him, but it didn't entirely work as her cheeks had gone pink.

'Damn you, Ben.'

He smiled, feeling wicked. 'So, what do you say?'

His hand was moving higher now, closer to the hot juncture between her legs. He was ruthless—but she wasn't stopping him from pushing her legs further apart.

He could feel her heat and smell her sweet, musky arousal, and the friction against her pert bottom only made things more acute. He shifted slightly, so that she could feel what she was doing to him.

By now her breath was choppy. He could feel the tension in her body as she fought not to give in to him. 'Just the weekend, you say?'

Ben wanted to growl at her insistence on putting boundaries in place, but he resisted the urge. In another couple of days all those boundaries would be gone.

'Yes, just the weekend.' He ignored his conscience. He'd seduced this woman into his bed—he could seduce her into marriage.

She looked at him for a long moment, with such intensity that Ben almost wanted to hide from her searing gaze, and then, abruptly, she moved. For a second Ben thought she was getting up to leave, but then she was lifting a leg over his lap and coming back down to straddle him.

Her robe had parted marginally and she moved her hips against him in a small undulating movement that made him bite back a curse as he felt her naked flesh press hotly against the erection straining against his trousers.

She cocked her head. 'Well, for starters, you're way too overdressed for a weekend of debauchery...'

And with that she reached for the hem of his top, pulling it up so that he had to raise his arms, and then it was off, landing on the floor.

She'd taken him by surprise again. Ben was so taken aback at her capitulation that he could only sit there for a moment, and then she grinned at him, bright and sudden, and he felt it like a punch in his gut. He also felt something constrict in his chest but he pushed it down, focusing on the physical.

He dislodged her hands with ease and pulled at the rest of her robe, baring those beautiful breasts to his gaze. He cupped them, dragging his thumbs across her stiffening nipples, and heard her sharp intake of breath.

By the time he'd licked and sucked those peaks to sharp wet points Lia was lifting herself up from his lap and fumbling with his trousers, freeing his aching arousal from its confinement. By the time he was sheathed with protection and embedded in her snug embrace they were both breathing as if they'd run a marathon, a glow of perspiration coating their skin.

Lia's robe was off, on the floor behind her, and Ben didn't even have any recollection of pushing it to the ground, the conflagration between them had been so swift and sudden. He surged up into her body, over and over, his arms welded tight across her back.

Lia pushed him right to the edge, and over, every time. Her face was flushed, she was biting her lip, and her eyes were glazed with passion… Ben realised with satisfaction that he was seeing her come undone, exactly as he'd imagined when he'd looked at her that first evening they'd met.

Except his sense of satisfaction was short-lived. Nothing in his imagination could have prepared him for this reality, or the sheer strength and awesome power of the climax that ripped through them within minutes of their bodies joining.

For a long moment in the aftermath Ben's head rested helplessly on Lia's breasts. She had her hands on his head, fingers funnelled deep into his hair, holding him there. He was still embedded deep in her body and he could feel the rhythmic post-orgasmic flutters of her body along his length.

He realised that even if he'd wanted to pull away from the embrace he couldn't.

When he finally was able to move he lifted his head and looked at her. The fact that she seemed similarly shattered was absurdly satisfying, but that was almost immediately followed by a sensation of uneasiness as Ben realised that whenever he'd believed he had her where he wanted her before, she'd eluded him.

He was a man who exerted control in all things, and he would make sure that didn't happen again. There was no room for failure here. Lia was an acquisition he couldn't afford to lose now.

'What day is it?' Lia said sleepily into the pillow as she felt a finger trace the bones of her spine.

Amazingly, her body tingled and she groaned. She heard a deep chuckle and wanted to scowl, but she didn't have the energy.

Mustering all the strength she did have, she

turned over, dislodging Ben's hand and pulling the sheet up over her body. She glared at him balefully.

He held up his hand, his face a picture of innocence. Well, if you could call his stubbled gorgeousness innocent. Which, of course, he wasn't—remotely. He was wicked, and he had made her do unspeakably wanton things for hours and hours; night had melted into dawn and then day, and then dusk and then night... And now it was getting dark outside again. The world might have ended and Lia wouldn't know.

'You didn't answer my question.'

Ben put his hands on either side of her body and leant over her, his chest broad and bare. 'It's Sunday evening—and I don't think I can take another Room Service meal.'

Lia reeled. She'd known what day it was—of course she had. But still... To hear him confirm that they'd passed almost three full days gorging on each other in a feast of the senses was overwhelming. She now knew, indelibly, that under Ben's expert touch she'd discovered her own sensuality and had learnt to revel in it. For that alone she'd lost a part of her soul to him.

She seized on his words, glad of an excuse to get out of this far too intimate space. 'I know a place near here...'

Ben smiled, and before Lia could stop him he'd whipped the sheet from her body. She squealed as he effortlessly lifted her into his arms. He strode into the bathroom and put her down to switch on the shower. She shivered with anticipation, unable to help herself.

Under the powerful spray of the water moments later, as Ben lathered shampoo into her hair and massaged her skull, Lia was glad she was facing away from him so he couldn't see her face. Because suddenly she felt bereft. It was Sunday evening and their weekend was almost over.

She'd left him behind in Bahia because she'd known that he'd slid under her skin...and now? Lia closed her eyes, as if that could help block out the suspicion that sliding under her skin was only the half of it. She was afraid she'd lost a whole lot more than a piece of her soul to Ben Carter.

He turned her around then and she kept her eyes closed, desperately telling herself, as his clever hands explored her slick body, that this was just lust clouding her brain and making her think crazy things.

For a moment she felt almost angry—that he'd managed to seduce her soul as well as her body so easily. Damn the man. She'd never wanted to go the way of her father—crippled by rejection. Not that Ben would even reject Lia—oh, no, she couldn't imagine him being so crass. He would do it with a silky touch and a devastating kiss and leave her reeling, wondering what had just happened…

But now Ben was sliding his hands between her legs, finding where her body was her ultimate betrayer and saying, 'Look at me, Lia.'

So, even though it was the last thing she wanted to do, she welcomed the distraction from her whirling, dangerous thoughts and assured herself that she would be fine. And she opened her eyes and kept them on him even as he tipped her over the edge and she screamed out her release… even as she was afraid that her worst fears would manifest in spite of everything.

CHAPTER EIGHT

LIA MIGHT HAVE regretted bringing Ben to her favourite restaurant if she hadn't been so hungry and in a physically weakened state from an overload of pleasure.

She took in the exposed stone walls covered with sepia-toned pictures of Italian scenes, slightly mottled with age. The small tables covered with checked tablecloths and the small vases filled with fake posies of flowers.

Feeling defensive, even though he looked remarkably at ease and delicious, dressed casually in faded jeans and a light woollen jumper, Lia said, 'I'm sure you're used to more salubrious establishments…but it's unpretentious and the food is to die for.'

Ben looked at her and smiled that wicked smile. It was as if he'd reached out and stroked her skin with his finger.

'If I'd known you were such a cheap date I'd have taken you to Jersey shore instead of Bahia.'

Lia's pulse tripped at his teasing.

And then he leaned forward and said conspiratorially, 'I'll have you know that I spent many a weekend serving margherita pizzas, and lasagne, to hungry New Yorkers while I worked my way through college.'

Lia seized on the opening he'd given her. 'How did you get to college?'

'As a kid from a foster home?'

She half shrugged and nodded. He knew she wasn't a snob, that she hadn't meant it like that. But she *was* curious to know how he'd begun his climb to the top.

Their starters had been served, and Ben took a bite from his *calamari fritti*, and wiped his mouth. 'After my parents died I was sent to my first foster home in Queens.'

Lia frowned. 'There were no friends or family who could take you in?'

A hard gleam came into Ben's eyes, turning them cold. Lia repressed a shiver and remembered what he'd said about people turning their backs on his parents after the scandal.

'My parents were both only children, and their own parents were dead. My mother had trouble conceiving. I was the result of years of IVF treatment.'

Lia took some of her soup but didn't taste it. Her whole attention was on Ben. She put down her spoon. 'What was it like…after they died?'

He looked at her. Strong, formidable. It was hard to imagine this man ever being vulnerable.

'It was tough…but it was almost a relief. They'd both fallen to pieces in the aftermath of the scandal. My father had become a bitter drunk. I used to come home from school, after another beating for my accent and different mannerisms and the fact that I was way ahead of everyone else in my class, to find him passed out on the couch. My mother was totally helpless. A Long Island princess living a nightmare. I had to do everything for them.' His jaw tightened. 'But that wasn't what bothered me the most—it was the fact that they gave up so easily.'

Lia tried to ignore the tightening in her chest. 'You got beaten up for your accent?'

He nodded. 'Every day. Until I realised that I had to fight back. And I did. I learned to blend in. By the time my parents died no one from my previous school would have recognised me.' He looked at her with a warning light in his eyes. 'It's not a pretty story, Lia.'

'If you think I'm looking for pretty stories then you still don't have a clue who I am,' she fired back.

Ben shook his head, an enigmatic look in his eyes. 'Tell me again why it is that you're not sunning yourself on some millionaire's yacht and worrying about tan lines?'

She arched a brow. 'That's the only choice open to me, is it? I could ask the same of you—you've surely earned enough by now…'

Ben lifted his glass, mouth quirking, 'I deserve that. *Touché.*'

When he stayed silent, though, still waiting for an answer, Lia said, 'I told you—it's never been what interests me. I was always nerdy at school—more interested in studying than in gossip or clothes—which didn't exactly earn me lots of friends.'

Ben tilted his head to one side, with a look in his eyes that she didn't quite like. 'Why is it that I get the impression that you were a shy kid? You were shy that evening up on the podium at the auction too.'

Lia sucked in a breath. Was she so awfully transparent to him? His perspicacity made her feel vulnerable.

He was waiting for her answer, and she was tempted to laugh it off, but then she found herself admitting, 'I *was* shy as a child. Cripplingly so. I had a stammer. And I used to blush all the time.' She desisted from revealing her mother's intolerance of that.

'But you got over it,' Ben said, and she heard the admiration in his voice.

Lia shrugged. 'I had to. I couldn't let it blight me.'

Their main courses arrived, and Lia seized the opportunity to divert his far too perceptive gaze from her, saying, 'You still haven't told me how you got to college.'

He gave her a look that told her explicitly that he didn't normally accept this level of grilling from anyone, but she just raised her brow again. He'd grilled *her*, and he'd comprehensively upended her life—this was the least she deserved.

Eventually he sighed and said, 'It started with a

cop—an Irish/American called Clancy. He picked a bunch of us up one day. By the age of sixteen I was in a gang. We were on our way to becoming serious delinquents—cutting school, shoplifting. I hadn't come on his radar before, so he looked into my background. When he found out where I'd come from he took me aside and laid it on the line. He told me that I'd already had more of a chance than any of those other kids, and that I was squandering the legacy my parents had given me.'

Ben shook his head.

'I was hard work by then—seriously angry and bitter with the world. He almost didn't get through to me…but he persuaded me to take part in a mentoring programme where local businessmen took on kids for internships. I ended up working as an intern for a local construction guy, and that was the start of it. I got out of the gang…stayed out of trouble as much as I could. It helped that I'd got moved to a more stable foster family. When I graduated from high school my mentor helped me get a scholarship to college and I did my basic degree. From that moment on I spent every minute either waiting tables or working on construction sites all over New York, and as soon as I got an opportunity I took it and didn't look back.'

Lia absorbed this and tried not to let herself picture the young angry teen at war with the world around him and grieving for so much. She knew instinctively that Ben wouldn't appreciate it. So instead she forked up a piece of her *carpaccio* and said lightly, 'Is *that* all?'

Ben just looked at her—and then he threw back his head and let out a sharp laugh. When he looked back at her there was something like grudging respect in his eyes and her chest expanded with a rush of emotion. *Dangerous.*

He shook his head. 'You never fail to surprise me, Miss Ford.'

She smiled back, even though the realisation of how happy it made her to make him laugh scared the life out of her. 'I try.'

His eyes narrowed on her then, and he said, 'So, why do you protect your father so much?'

Lia put down her fork, immediately feeling defensive. 'It's always been just the two of us...' She hesitated, and then said, 'After my mother left he never really recovered. For years he's suffered ill health, and I've always suspected it's mental as much as physical.'

'You can't take up the slack for him for ever.'

'I know that,' Lia said, the habitual weight of her father's expectations resting on her shoulders.

Ben was looking at her, and for a second she allowed herself a very illicit daydream of what it would be like to lean on someone else... But she ruthlessly shut it down.

The waiter appeared beside them, breaking the tension, and without looking at the man Ben said, 'We'll take the cheque, please.'

Lia felt relieved that Ben wasn't going to say any more about her father. Emotions she never usually allowed room to breathe were rising inside her, and when Ben held his hand out for hers, after leaving money on the table, she gave it without hesitation.

The cold air outside the restaurant didn't help with restoring her sense of equilibrium. It was as if Ben had unlocked a box and now everything was spilling out—everything she'd kept locked up for years. For ever.

He turned to her, his face lean and beautifully stark in the early-evening light. 'Lia—'

She reached up and put her hand over his mouth. His breath was warm against her palm. 'Just kiss me, Ben.'

She was afraid that if she said any more she would want more than he was offering. He put his hand over hers and pressed a kiss to her palm, and then he pulled her in close, right into his body, and kissed her deeply and thoroughly. It was as effective a way as any to block out the thoughts and feelings she wasn't prepared to inspect. *Yet.*

Ben seemed perfectly happy to avoid talking too, bundling her into a taxi before things got too heated in the middle of the busy street. The atmosphere in the back of the taxi was thick with sexual tension, and by the time they eventually reached the hotel suite again they couldn't even make it to the bedroom, stopping at the first soft surface, their urgency so frantic that when it was over Lia realised that they were both still partially dressed.

By the time they did make it to the bedroom, and Ben took off the rest of her clothes as reverently as if she was made of china, Lia knew that she was in serious trouble. No amount of distracting sex was going to keep the emotions and thoughts bubbling just under the surface at bay.

Lia was luxuriating in a hot bath early the following morning, while Ben was taking some calls on his phone, dressed fetchingly in nothing but a towel. She could get used to this decadent lifestyle, she thought to herself, as long as the Pandora's Box of emotions she'd been avoiding dealing with since the previous evening stayed locked away.

But it was too late for that.

Lia wanted to submerge herself under the water, block everything out, make it muffled. But she couldn't. Despite the warm water and luxurious oils she was tense, and her belly was tight.

It was as if a Benjamin Carter–shaped whirlwind had stormed into her life and ripped everything apart, throwing it all in the air, and now Lia wasn't sure where she fitted any more. Or even who she was.

Reluctantly she got out of the bath, her skin already wrinkling like a prune. Wiping the mirror clear, she sucked in a breath at her pink-cheeked reflection. She almost didn't recognise herself.

MARRIED FOR THE TYCOON'S EMPIRE

Her hair was tied up and long tendrils clung to her cheeks and forehead. Her eyes were wide and troubled-looking, but also suspiciously dreamy. She could see marks on her pale skin from where Ben had touched her with his mouth or his hands, and it automatically sent a carnal thrill through her blood.

Her hand curled around the edge of the sink, as if that might stop her flying apart when she thought properly of just how comprehensively Ben Carter had seduced her.

After this weekend she couldn't keep on fooling herself that it was purely physical for her... but what about for Ben?

Just then a knock on the door made her jump. She called out, 'Yes?'

'I'm going to run out to that French patisserie we spotted last night—do you want anything?'

Lia's heart was pounding. 'Just a croissant, thanks.'

'Okay—back in ten.'

Lia waited till she heard the faint sound of the main suite door closing and then she emerged and dressed quickly in the jeans and silk shirt that Ben had ordered for her on that first morning-after.

A little desperate now, she tried to count all the mornings-after—and couldn't. It was as if time had stopped and they were locked in this bubble.

Lia began pacing up and down, trying to calm herself. She couldn't seem to stop thinking about the fact that perhaps there was more for Ben too. He'd told her so much last night, and his reluctance had revealed that he didn't usually let people in.

He wasn't following his usual pattern with lovers, if the gossip was to be believed. Did a man who just wanted a brief fling cross the Atlantic to find out more about a woman?

Against all Lia's most hardened instincts, she felt a flutter of illicit excitement in her gut. Perhaps…just perhaps…this was *more*. And perhaps Ben wouldn't just jet off back to New York. Then something sank inside her. And yet how could it work when they lived on different continents? How could she leave her father?

Her thoughts were racing so much that Lia put her hands to her cheeks and they were hot. A semi-hysterical giddiness rose up inside her. And hope. And a kind of euphoria. She was falling for Ben…

After the weekend they'd just shared, she couldn't believe that what he felt for her was purely physical...and she couldn't believe that she was even thinking about risking her worst fears. But right now, with Ben's taste still on her lips and his touch like a brand on her skin, she felt absurdly confident and a little invincible.

Just then there was a sound at the suite door and Lia went to investigate, finding that a selection of the day's newspapers had been pushed underneath. Ben must have requested them. Automatically she bent to pick them up, only half taking in the headlines—until one jumped out at her and the rest of the papers dropped to the floor, unnoticed.

American construction tycoon follows construction heiress back to England after million-dollar weekend in Brazil! Can Julianna Ford be the one to tame Ben Carter's wild ways?

Under the headline was a grainy picture of Ben and Lia, kissing in the street the previous evening. It was just before they'd got into the cab. They hadn't even noticed. There were also fuzzy shots of them eating dinner. Immediately the memory was tarnished.

Lia felt sick and walked back into the living area and sat on the edge of a chair. It was only to be expected that someone as high-profile as Ben Carter would be tracked and followed, but for Lia, who'd never fallen foul of the tabloids, it was a shock to see her name in print like this.

She kept reading even though she didn't want to, frowning when she saw another picture that was familiar because she'd seen it before. It was of Ben and the three other tycoons, emerging from that private club in Manhattan some weeks before.

There was renewed speculation as to why the men had met up in Manhattan that night, and if it had something to do with reversing the negative press attention they'd all been receiving. And there was a lewd suggestion that Ben Carter was hoping to swap more than just bodily fluids with Lia, considering her own family background.

Lia thought of her father seeing this paper and barely managed to keep from rushing to the bathroom to be sick. The thought was literally nauseating.

Just then Lia heard a chiming noise and looked

to see her mobile phone on a nearby table. Her gut clenched with dread at the thought that it would be her father because he'd seen the article, but she frowned when she saw the name at the top of the text: Dante Mancini. He was the Italian tycoon Ben had been meeting that night in Manhattan, along with Xander Trakas and Sheikh Zayn Al-Ghamdi. Why would he be texting her? And how did he even have her number?

The words of the message jumped out at her.

Have you seen the papers, Carter? Looks like your million-dollar gamble is paying off. You might just beat the rest of us to the altar—

The rest of the message was hidden unless she unlocked the phone, and it was only when she tried to do so and it wouldn't unlock that the significance of the fact that it was addressed to Ben finally sank in—this wasn't her phone. It was exactly the same model, but it was Ben's.

The implication of the message was too confusing and potentially huge to take in at first. Words reverberated in Lia's head: *gamble...altar...beat the rest of us.* That picture of them emerging from the club loomed in her mind's eye now. Almost accusatory.

She recalled her initial meeting with Ben and how suspicious she'd been, and how somehow along the way she'd forgotten about that. Her conscience mocked her. *Somehow?* Her suspicion had been forgotten in a blaze of heat so intense she still felt scorched.

She looked at that photo again, a sick kind of dread churning in her belly. They all looked so grim and intent.

The fledgling tender emotions Lia had been feeling seemed to shrivel inside her. She had the very sick suspicion that she was the most monumental fool in the world.

She, of all people, who had seen how cruel and ruthless people could be. Even those who were meant to love you the most. She who had learnt her lesson, but had been all too ready to forget everything and believe in an illusion.

And just then she heard the sounds heralding Ben's return from the bakery.

When Ben walked into the suite's main foyer he saw the newspapers on the floor, where they'd fallen. He sensed instantly that something was wrong—like in Bahia, when he'd woken to find Lia gone. He stepped over them and his mouth tightened. If she'd run out on him again, like she had before...

But he came to a halt in the doorway of the living area when he saw her standing with her back to him at the main window. The relief that rushed through him would be worrying if he hadn't still been feeling uneasy.

'Hey, I've got some pastries and croissants.'

Lia didn't turn around straight away, and when she did he saw her face was set. Pale. Her arms were crossed in a clearly defensive gesture. A million miles from the sleep-flushed woman who had smiled as he'd kissed her awake earlier...

Ben put down the bag on a nearby table. The way Lia was looking at him made him feel more wary than concerned. 'Did something happen?'

'You could say that,' she answered tonelessly.

Ben frowned, but before he could respond to ask her *What?* she spoke again.

'What is this, Ben? What are we doing here?'

A million carnal images came into his mind, but he desisted from making any facetious comment.

An awful suspicion was entering his head—*she knows…somehow she knows.*

'What do you think this is, Lia?'

She looked at him for a long moment. 'To be perfectly honest, I'm not sure. It's an elaborate seduction—that much I do know. For someone who up till just weeks ago was a perennial bachelor with a tarnished playboy status.'

Now Ben flushed, and gritted his jaw. 'You didn't seem interested in analysing things before now.'

'No.' Lia sounded bitter. 'More fool me.'

His gut clenched in rejection of that. 'You're not a fool, Lia.'

She arched a brow. 'No?'

Then she reached down for the newspaper on the couch near her and lobbed it over to Ben, who caught it on a reflex. He saw the headline and felt inordinately relieved.

Barely skimming the article and photo, he looked at her. 'Is this all?' It was just the tabloids…if anything this would work in Ben's favour.

'No, that's not all.' Lia's tone was even cooler now. 'You got a text message from a friend. I mistakenly read some of it because I thought it was my phone. But I'm not sorry I read it. I found it quite illuminating.'

Ben saw his phone on a table nearby and picked it up. When he saw the message he unlocked his phone to read it all the way to the end.

You might just beat the rest of us to the altar, so enjoy your freedom while you can. Ciao. Mancini.

Ben could almost hear the man's drawling, sarcastic tone and he had to restrain himself from hurling the phone against something solid.

When he looked at Lia she was even paler, and her eyes were like two stark blue sapphires. Swirling with anger and other things he couldn't decipher.

'Why did he call it a million-dollar gamble?'

Something solid and heavy settled in Ben's chest. He really hadn't wanted it to go like this, but perhaps it was better just to be completely brutally honest. He threw the paper and his phone down.

He funnelled a hand through his hair and looked at Lia. 'I initiated a meeting with the others after the press seemed to have become intent on decimating our reputations. There's a charity we're all involved in, and it was beginning to be adversely affected. That was the breaking point for me. I figured that if Trakas, Mancini and Sheikh Al-Ghamdi would agree to join forces with me, we could beat the press at their own game.'

Lia's voice was tight. 'So you had your meeting and what…? Discussed strategies?'

Ben felt grim. 'Something like that.'

She said nothing for a moment, but Ben could almost hear her brain whirring. She was a smart woman. It wouldn't take her long. And it didn't. Her eyes grew wider and her face was leached of the little colour that had come into it.

'You set up that date with me a week after your meeting. What's the betting that if I was to call Elizabeth Young now she'd tell me that you all signed up with her?'

Ben had to admit it. 'She would tell you that, yes. We did all sign up with her. And we signed up with her because we decided that our best course of action would be to clean up our reputations by…settling down.'

Lia gaped at him. Her eyes were huge. Faintly she said, 'I can't believe it… You made some sort of sick pact to find women and get married to prove that you're all moving on from your playboy images?'

Feeling tight all over, Ben said, 'People get married for less every day of the week.'

Lia's eyes blazed at him now. He wasn't even sure if she'd heard what he'd said.

'No wonder he called your million-dollar bid a gamble. Were you hoping I'd become completely infatuated with you? Or were you just going to pop the question after testing out our physical compatibility?'

Something on Ben's face must have given him away, because Lia stepped back, shaking her head. There was a light in her eyes that skewered Ben to the spot, all at once accusatory and something more ambiguous.

'To think that I suspected you had an agenda right from the start… But even I could never have guessed you'd go so far.'

The only thing anchoring Lia to the ground was the intense anger she felt. She told herself it wasn't hurt and betrayal. She told herself the feelings she'd believed were real just a short while before had been just a flight of fancy and brought on by sex hormones. How could she have fallen for this man?

She cursed herself for not having trusted her gut at the start. For letting Ben fool her into thinking… Her heart stuttered—thinking what? That he cared for her? What a travesty! Clearly all he cared about was his precious business and his reputation.

Where had her healthy sense of cynicism gone? Melted, she thought disgustedly, along with her will power as soon as he'd touched her… But worse than anything else at that moment was the hurt she felt that he'd lied to her when he'd told her in Brazil that he'd wanted her after just looking at her photo, before he'd even known who she was. And she hated herself for being so weak.

Ben just looked at her, assessing her reaction. He seemed remote, a million miles from the seductive lover who had sent her to heaven and back more times than she cared to admit.

'You were prepared to marry once before for convenience,' Ben pointed out.

Lia felt even sicker now, when she thought of all she'd revealed to him. When all along he'd been playing her like a virtuoso. She lifted her chin and tried to ignore the sensation of something cracking apart in her chest. It was anger, she told herself desperately.

'Yes, I was. But I was misguided and doing it for all the wrong reasons.'

'We have more going for us than you ever did with your ex-fiancé. We have insane chemistry. We have ambitions and goals in common. We could build a good life together.'

To hear him so baldly laying out exactly what he'd had in mind all along was like a body-blow. And Lia realised for the first time that she'd changed. She might have agreed to a marriage of convenience before, for her father's sake and on a subconscious level to protect herself from the pain of intimacy, but she'd never do it again. She knew she was worth more than that now. And the fact that it was this man who'd given her that sense of self was galling.

Ben continued, 'I can take care of you and your father. You've admitted his health is failing, Lia. It's only a matter of time before he has to step down. You can't go on protecting him for ever.

You can't go on sacrificing your own ambitions for his.'

Lia hated him even more for being able to strike at the very heart of her. She'd given him that power. This was what happened when you let people in. They knew where your weak points were and she'd all but given Ben a map and directions. She had no one but herself to blame. She shouldn't have stopped listening to her suspicions.

She bristled at the implication that she needed taking care of. 'Wow, you must have *really* thought you had it all sorted when you spotted me in the Leviathan portfolio. Not only could you get your convenient wife, you could also be assured of further expansion into Europe.'

Colour scored along Ben's cheeks, but Lia didn't feel triumphant to have scored a hit—she felt worse...disappointed. Betrayed. She couldn't keep denying it.

He said, 'I'd make sure that your father's business thrives, that his name survives. You'd want for nothing.'

Lia tightened her arms around herself as if that might hold her together. 'What you're describing is a business merger—and were you not listening when I told you that wealth and all its trappings mean nothing to me?'

Ben's jaw clenched. 'That's easy to say when you haven't had it all ripped away and seen the effect on your family.'

Lia was momentarily rendered speechless. He was right, in one way. Even if she knew that she could survive, she knew something like what had happened to his parents would kill her father. And she hated it that even now her heart ached a little for what had happened to Ben... She hated that she wanted to ask him if he'd felt anything at all beyond this absurd plan. But she wouldn't. She wasn't a complete masochist. And he'd just revealed a level of ruthlessness that took her breath away.

'I'm not interested in a marriage of convenience with you, Benjamin Carter.'

A muscle ticked in his jaw. 'And yet you were prepared to live a lie of a life with a man who left you completely cold?'

Terrified he'd guess what a personal revelation she'd had, she fired back, 'I'd rather have *that* life than one with a man who would seduce his way to getting what he wants…lying with his body and his touch. You disgust me.'

You disgust me.

Something snapped inside Ben—some control he'd been clinging to. Something that had made him feel impotent in the face of her accusations. She was right…he *had* set out to woo her with marriage in mind…but she didn't know that he'd almost forgotten that objective, that he'd found it so much more preferable to lose himself in her. Over and over again.

'You still want me,' he ground out, feeling feral. Feeling desperate.

She shook her head, eyes wide, icy. 'No.'

Her denial pushed Ben over the edge of his control. He closed the distance between them in two long strides and reached for her, wrapping his hands around her arms and tugging her towards him. She tipped up her chin mutinously, her arms still locked across her chest, pushing up the tantalising swells of her breasts under the silk shirt.

There was a hint of panic in her voice. 'This means nothing, Ben. Just because I might react—'

He stopped the rest of her words with his mouth,

crushing all that tart sweetness, hauling her close to his chest. They were locked for long seconds in a tense embrace and then Ben gentled his hold. His hand reached for her head, fingers tangling in her hair. His other hand slid down her arm, and then to her waist.

For a long second she did nothing, and Ben expected her to pull away, but then, with something that sounded halfway between a sob and a moan, she softened and opened her mouth.

Exultation rose swiftly in Ben's blood, drowning out the self-recrimination and guilt. He knew only this…her delicious curves melting into him…her tongue touching his.

They kissed frantically, passionately. Angrily. Her arms slid around his neck and her body bowed into his. Ben's hands cupped her buttocks through her jeans and he notched his body against the juncture of her legs.

He was about to lift her up and hook her legs around his waist, so he could take her into the bedroom, when suddenly she stiffened and then pulled out of his arms. They were both breathing harshly and she was looking at him as if he'd just kicked a puppy.

She shook her head and said harshly, 'No, I don't want this, Ben. I want more than just a convenient marriage and a mutual lust which will inevitably burn itself out. And then where would that leave us? It's all a lie.'

Blood was pumping to Ben's erogenous zones and away from his brain. It was hard to think straight. He had to exert extreme control over his body. 'It's not a lie. It's the most honesty I've ever felt in my life.'

Lia shook her head again and started to walk away, into the bedroom. The fact that she seemed to be unsteady on her feet, which showed how much he'd affected her, was no comfort. He wasn't sure he was so steady himself.

She emerged minutes later, carrying the big designer bag that had come with the clothes he'd ordered. She walked quickly to the door, avoiding his eye.

An awful mix of panic and desperation made Ben say, 'So? What? You're saying that you want more now? After everything you've experienced?'

She stopped at the door, her hand on the knob. She turned around and something gripped Ben. She looked very young and delicate, her mouth swollen after his kiss. He wanted to feel it under his again. *For ever.*

She lifted her chin and in that moment she looked almost regal. 'Maybe I do. Maybe I'm not as cynical as I thought. I'm certainly not as cynical as you. And, apart from anything else, I could never trust you.' Then she said, 'I'd appreciate it if you wouldn't go after my father.'

It took a second for her words to register, and then Ben felt like snarling. Clearly her opinion of him was still low, no matter what confidences they'd shared, or these recent revelations.

Tautly he assured her, 'Your father won't be hearing from me. But that doesn't mean he won't be a target for others.'

'Maybe,' she said. 'But we'll deal with that if and when it happens.'

Ben felt an almost violent surge of protectiveness—*he* wanted to deal with it if it happened. He didn't want Lia to be the one standing between her father and some unscrupulous shark. And then he realised that she believed that shark was him.

She was opening the door before he could react and then she was gone...only the faintest perfume lingering behind her. Ben felt numb, in spite of the residual hum of arousal in his blood. The taste of her mouth was still on his tongue.

For a second he couldn't breathe. He turned around and went to the window, his gaze latching on to the soaring buildings, reminding him of what was important. What was solid.

He would be true to his word. He wouldn't go after her father. Ben's mouth firmed. There were others he could target; he wouldn't let this stand in his way. And as for the original plan to find a bride…? Nothing had changed.

The sooner he put Lia Ford into the past and got his life back on track, the better.

He waited until he was on his way to the airport a little later that morning before he made the call. When Elizabeth Young answered and realised who it was, she wasted no time in telling Ben what she thought of him going behind her back to pursue Lia anyway.

When she'd stopped speaking, Ben delivered his piece and then bit out, 'Can you set me up on another date? Please?'

After a long moment she said, 'You have one

more chance, Mr Carter, but only because I know how hard it is for men like you to admit you were wrong and to say *please*.'

CHAPTER NINE

'WOW, YOU'RE ACTUALLY admitting you want a marriage of convenience—that's pretty cold.' The woman Ben had had three very chaste dates with over the past two weeks—because he couldn't bring himself to even think about kissing her—seemed to absorb that for a moment and then said, 'I'd have to consider it—and see the prenuptial agreement, of course—but it's certainly a possibility.'

Ben wasn't even surprised that she wasn't running away as if he was a two-headed monster. He'd dated enough hard-nosed and cynical women in New York to know that many wouldn't balk at a proposal like this. To some it would be positively romantic.

The woman who sat on the opposite side of the dinner table to Ben, in one of Manhattan's most exclusive restaurants, was stunningly beautiful.

Blonde, and groomed to within an inch of her life. A UN interpreter.

She'd make a perfect wife—on paper, at least. But the fact that the union he sought was potentially within his grasp left him utterly unmoved. Because he knew it wasn't going to happen.

He was haunted by someone else. *Lia.* He'd thought he could excise her from his life, move on. The reality was somewhat less...facile. It was downright impossible, in fact, and as the days passed it got worse. Not better. Even now he burned. For *her.* He would have her over any amount of suitable women and she could walk out on him as much as she liked...he'd always go after her.

A sense of bleak futility gripped him and he put down his napkin, saying, 'I'm sorry about wasting your time, but actually this isn't going to work.'

A look of alarm came over his date's face. 'Look, I'm willing to think it over.'

Ben felt grim. 'I'm sorry, but, no.'

She put down her napkin too, and exasperation was evident on her face. She stood up and looked down at him. 'If you want my advice, go and deal with whatever or whoever has you tied up in knots. If you still want to talk then, give me a call. I won't wait around for ever, though,' she added warningly, just before she walked out.

Ben threw down some money on the table, disgusted with himself, and left too, walking out into the cool night air, hands deep in the pockets of his overcoat.

He walked for block after block, until he found himself down near the wrecking site of an old building he'd just acquired. They'd knocked it down just that day. A hoarding emblazoned with his name blocked the view of the mound of rubble. The building had been two hundred years old and crumbling. But for the first time in his life he felt a pang. It had had history—people had lived and died there. It had witnessed lives. And now it was gone, reduced to nothing.

It would be replaced by something new, modern. A skyscraper, making the most out of a small space. Progress. Development. Moving on. So why did Ben feel so damn empty when at this point he usually felt nothing but satisfaction flowing through his veins?

He turned around, emitting something like a

growl, making a couple passing near him look at him warily.

Oblivious to their reaction, Ben looked around him at all the darkened buildings, empty but for a few cleaners. They were solid—shining symbols of the resurrection and success he'd always strived to achieve, something he could literally reach out and touch—but ultimately they were no safer than the building he'd had demolished today. They were just as fragile, susceptible to being destroyed.

From here he could see the twin beams of light marking Ground Zero. If anything signified the fragility of structures and life, that did. But it also symbolised strength and fortitude and survival. A contradiction.

For the first time in his life Ben had a sense that even if he lost everything tomorrow he would be able to get back up and build it all again. After all, he'd started from nothing. He wasn't his father—he would never collapse and disappear as he had done. Or his mother.

He felt something lift off his shoulders...some weight he hadn't even noticed. He faced back the way he'd come, filled with a sense of resolve.

He knew he'd made a pact with Mancini, Trakas and Sheikh Al-Ghamdi, but suddenly what had mattered all those weeks ago didn't any more. Ben knew now that he could only go one way and suffer the consequences…no matter what they might be.

A week later

Lia was standing at the window in her office, looking out over London broodingly. The weather matched her mood: grey and wet. She imagined Ben Carter in his beautiful villa in Bahia, seducing his latest possible wife, the stunning blonde she'd seen in pictures alongside breathless speculation that this woman might be the one to tame the mercurial tycoon.

A knife twisted in her guts and Lia sucked in a breath.

She couldn't deny it any more. She couldn't keep telling herself that she hadn't really been falling for him. That it had just been hormones.

She was in love with the man. Deeply. Irrevocably. But she didn't regret walking away from him. No wonder she'd agreed to a marriage of convenience with Simon—it had been eminently safe! But a marriage of convenience with a man she had feelings for…? That would be pure torture. He only wanted her for the advancement she could offer to his reputation and business. Once again his sheer ruthlessness made her suck in a painful breath.

She scowled at her reflection in the glass, hating it that she looked wan and tired after sleepless nights full of X-rated dreams. She loved him—but she hated him for his betrayal and ruthless calculation.

Just then her mobile rang and she turned around, sighing deeply. She saw the name on the display and picked it up, forcing a smile so she didn't sound as miserable as she felt.

'Dad! Is everything okay?'

He'd been instructed to work from home this past week, to help his rehabilitation, but Lia knew he'd been impatient to get back into his office in town, where she worked too. Thankfully he'd never mentioned the tabloid splash about her and Ben, so he couldn't have seen it.

They chatted for a few minutes and then he said, 'Actually, I had a visitor this morning.'

Lia asked idly, 'You did? Who?'

Her father cleared his throat and said, 'Benjamin Carter, the American construction mogul...'

Lia went very still. She could feel her hand tightening on the phone and her blood draining south.

Her father was still talking, and she interrupted him in shock. 'He did *what?*'

'He asked for your hand in marriage. And we spoke about a possible merger... He's right, you know, Lia. I'm not getting any younger or healthier. You have your own ambitions. I need to be practical...'

Lia sat down heavily in a chair, as shocked to hear him mention her ambitions as to hear about his visitor. 'I'm so sorry, Dad. It's all my fault... We met in New York and he pursued me... But he only ever wanted me because of your company, and he needs a wife, and—' Lia closed her mouth abruptly before she said too much. She could feel the shock wearing off, to be replaced by hot, molten emotion. Ben had gone behind her back and done what she'd expressly asked him not to.

'I see...' said her father. 'And how do you feel about him?'

'I hate him,' Lia said quickly, even as a voice said, *Liar, liar, pants on fire.*

'Lia, look, I don't think you really understand—'

'No, Dad.' She cut him off. 'Listen, this is all my fault. I'm going to take care of it.'

She cut the connection before her father could say anything else. Then reached for her office phone and asked her PA to get her Ben's UK office address.

No way was Ben Carter going to get away with this. The fact that she felt butterflies at the thought of seeing him again was as irritating as hell, but she ignored it.

Lia wasn't quite prepared to see Ben striding towards her in the lobby of his very modern steel office building in central London. He looked fierce and intent, but stopped in his tracks as soon as he saw her.

'*Lia.*'

For a bizarre second he looked at her as if she was a ghost. But then he blinked and said, 'I was just coming to see you.'

She folded her arms over her chest and tried to ignore the pounding of her heart. 'Well, I've saved you a trip. Did you seriously think I'd let this go?'

Ben frowned, and Lia noticed for the first time

that he looked a little more unkempt than usual. And tired. Lines she hadn't noticed before had appeared around his mouth.

Churlishly she figured it must be hard work, vetting a new wife. Even if he wasn't in Bahia right now. A skewer pierced deep to remind her of how easy she'd been to seduce.

'What did your father tell you?'

'All I needed to know—which is that you came to him talking about mergers and acquisitions. And that you asked for my hand in marriage.'

Anger and renewed betrayal boiled over when she thought of revealing to him how much her father wanted her to settle down.

She stepped closer and hissed at him. 'How could you? You deliberately took a confidence I shared with you and used it to your advantage.'

She only realised she was too close when his distinctive scent reached her nostrils, impacting on her starved hormones. But she wouldn't back away now and show him that he affected her at all. She lifted her chin, challenging him.

'I take it that you didn't let your father explain everything I said, then?'

Now Lia blinked. Her father *had* been saying

something when she'd cut him off. She ignored the dart of doubt. 'I heard all I needed to. What possible other explanation could there be for your presence here in England?'

Ben's eyes glittered. 'What, indeed?'

Lia became aware that people were walking through the foyer and trying desperately not to look as if they were eavesdropping.

Ben obviously realised the same and cursed. 'We can't have this conversation here.'

He'd taken her by the arm and was walking towards a set of lifts before Lia could respond. She started to try to pull free. 'I think we've said all we need to say,' she hissed. 'You need to leave me and my father alone—you're not going to get what you want.'

But in spite of her words and efforts she was in the lift with him now, and he was pressing a button and they were ascending.

He let her go once they were moving and said grimly, 'You're not leaving until you hear what I have to say.'

Lia glared at him, struck temporarily mute as she was bombarded with memories of what had happened in a lift before. Mutual combustion. As if he were remembering the same thing Ben's eyes darkened, and his gaze dropped to her breasts under her silk shirt before lazily coming back up again. Lia could feel damp heat bloom between her legs, mere seconds after meeting the man again. She wanted to scream at the control he still had over her body.

But now the doors were opening and she could see they were on the top floor. Ben all but pulled her out of the lift and marched her down a long corridor with glass cube offices either side. People tried frantically to look uninterested as they passed by. Lia debated screaming, but then imagined Ben putting his mouth on hers to keep her quiet…

He took her to an office at the end—the largest one—with wraparound views of London and the dark brown Thames snaking through the iconic buildings on either side. It was impressive.

But not as impressive as the man who shut the door behind him and planted himself in front of it, his powerful body blocking her exit. Damn him.

Lia backed away. 'What the hell do you want, Mr Carter? I don't have time for this.'

He smiled mirthlessly as he leant back against

the door, hands in his trouser pockets. 'I see we've gone back to Mr Carter.'

Lia folded her arms, feeling vulnerable in this enclosed space, even if it was all windows. 'Well, what did you expect?'

A look of something like self-recrimination passed over Ben's face, and then he pushed off the door and went to stand at the window, looking out. His back was broad, and Lia couldn't help remembering that day in Bahia, when he'd been working on the roof of the villa, laughing and joking with Esmé's husband.

She scowled. That man had never existed.

Ben spoke then, cutting through her acid recriminations. 'I was once told by a colleague that my buildings had more heart than me, and he was right. I believed that buildings weren't fallible and that my structures would keep standing even if I fell. They're not weakened by emotions and human frailty, or greed and corruption. Except…that's not true.'

Feeling a little disorientated, Lia said, 'What do you mean?'

After a long moment Ben turned around to face her. There was something bleak in his eyes. 'I was wrong to believe that my redemption lay in the structures I created and built.'

Lia shook her head, resisting the desire to understand him. 'I really couldn't care less about what you think of your buildings.'

Ben cursed softly and ran a hand through his hair, leaving it mussed up. He pinpointed her with that blue gaze.

'I'm trying to tell you…' He stopped. And then he spoke more forcibly. 'I did come to see your father to talk about the business, and to ask for your hand in marriage.'

Lia felt pain lance her. 'I know. Which is why—'

'But not in the way you think.'

She stopped talking and something started beating inside her. Butterflies again. Or her heart. Or something more dangerous…hope. Damn hope. It would survive a nuclear apocalypse.

'What, then?'

Ben's gaze seemed to be burning all the way into her. 'I came to tell him that I want to marry his daughter because…I love her.' He waited a beat, as if to let her absorb that, and then he said, watching her carefully, 'But I told him that she wouldn't believe me after what I did to her and so I had to somehow prove it to her. And the only way I knew how to do that was by asking your father to take *me* over. I want to prove to you that you're more important to me than everything I've built up, because it all means nothing without you.'

Lia wasn't sure if she was still standing. She struggled to understand, shaking her head faintly, 'But…you let me leave. And you've been dating… that woman.'

Ben grimaced. 'I was too proud to admit that you'd got to me on an emotional level. My life was never about emotions—it was about building structures that affirmed my place in the world. Rooting my security in something solid. I was in denial, determined to put you out of my mind and get on with my life.'

A rueful look flashed across his face then. 'I was also terrified… Suddenly nothing felt relevant or important any more. I felt as if I was going mad. I'd only ever trusted myself, and yet I couldn't trust my own instincts any more because every instinct was telling me to come back to you, to admit that my priorities had changed…completely. And nothing happened with that woman. She bored me to tears, and she wasn't you.'

Lia felt breathless, as if a huge fist was squeezing around her heart. The pressure was enormous. 'Even if I believed what you say about handing everything over to my father...even if I was to agree to marry you...ultimately you'd have everything anyway—you'd still have achieved what you wanted.'

His eyes were so blue it almost hurt to look at them. He was willing her to believe him—she could see that. But something was holding her back. *Fear*.

All she could see in her mind's eye was how her father had slowly diminished more and more as the years had passed and it had become less and less likely that Lia's mother would ever return. And now someone was standing in front of her, asking for her heart...and she was filled with terror.

She backed away, panic galvanising her. Emotion constricted her voice. 'I can't...do this.'

She whirled around, away from that too penetrating gaze, and made it to the door. She opened it just as her vision started to blur, but then it was slammed shut again and Ben was behind her, his hands above her head. Capturing her.

She turned around and looked up. He was too close. 'Let me *go.*'

He shook his head, looking fierce. 'Never.'

'I don't trust you—how can I?' Her heart was pumping nearly out of her chest.

Ben shook his head, caging her in. 'It's not me you don't trust—it's yourself. Because you're too afraid to reach out and grab what you've always denied yourself: the chance of the happiness you deserve. Just because your father denied it to himself his whole life, it doesn't mean you have to.'

His words struck deep into the very heart of her and Lia lashed out defensively. 'Since when did you become a psychologist?'

Ben's mouth quirked. 'Since a beautiful, bright, brave woman stalked away from our first date and turned my world upside down and inside out, showing me that everything I thought was important *wasn't.*'

Lia felt tears threaten. '*You* turned *my* world upside down and inside out.'

Ben's expression changed. Became serious. 'I know,' he said. 'Because from the moment I saw you I wanted you more than anything I've ever wanted before. Yes, I knew who you were, and, yes, I had an agenda. But in all honesty they were the last things on my mind. I had to keep reminding myself of my objective; that's why I let you go. I realised how far off course I'd come. I'd lost track of everything that I'd believed was important.'

His mouth tightened.

'When you walked away I told myself the last thing I needed was a wife who actually made me *feel* anything. I told you the truth when I told you I wanted you from first sight…as soon as I saw your photo I was done for. The fact that you were who you were…that made it justifiable for me to go after you. I will do whatever it takes to make you believe me, Lia. I will sign over Carter Construction to you, to your favourite charity, to Santa Claus…whoever you want. Trust me on this. My solicitor is just down the hall. Say the word and I'll have contracts drawn up. And I will never ask you to marry me if you're afraid that's still my endgame. If you can tell me that you truly don't want this, that you don't feel anything for me, then I'll let you go and you'll never hear from me again.'

Lia looked up into those blue eyes that had sent shockwaves through her as soon as she'd seen them. And all she could see was blazing determination, truth and...her heart hitched...*love*. This man was ready to destroy everything he'd built up—for her. And he hadn't lied about wanting her from the moment he'd seen her photo.

But there was still something holding her back.

Her voice was little more than a whisper. 'But how can I trust that you won't leave eventually? Or that you won't hurt me?'

Lia had literally nowhere to hide. She was laid bare, exposing her deepest fears.

Ben looked so fierce for a second that she sucked in a breath.

'I would never leave you. *Ever.* You have just as much power to hurt me—more.'

Lia felt something fierce rush through her at the thought of this man being hurt...of leaving him behind. 'I could never hurt you.'

Some expression crossed Ben's face, something almost like satisfaction, and then he said, 'Not everyone is like our parents, Lia. Some people do find happiness. Security. Do you love me?'

Without an atom left in her body capable of keeping up her high walls of defence, Lia just nodded.

'Well, then,' Ben said softly, his eyes turning suspiciously shiny, 'we're already different to them. Because I love you too, and I pledge here and now to do everything in my power to make you happy for as long as we live.'

Lia absorbed that.

And then Ben said, 'They didn't love each other, Lia, not really. Not your parents, nor my parents. And that's where they failed.'

She looked at him and her chest expanded. Was he right? Could things really be different for them because they loved each other? Could it really be that simple?

But she already knew the answer, deep in her core, because it was spreading outwards and infusing her whole body with a lightness she'd never felt before. It could be that simple…and that hard…because loving Benjamin Carter was the scariest thing she'd ever done in her life. And the easiest.

And so she did the only thing she could. She reached up and pulled Ben's face down to hers and kissed him, until all the doubts and fears had fled and there was only love left behind.

Much later, in a hotel room around the corner from Ben's offices, Lia lay sated and blissfully drowsy after reuniting with Ben in a very comprehensive and convincing manner. She was tucked close in to his side, his arm around her. He was not letting her escape—not that she had any intention of doing that.

She trailed her finger up and down his chest, lazily, and after a while lifted her head to look at him. He looked back at her with slumberous blue eyes, a sexy smile making his mouth quirk.

'You know how you said you'd never ask me to marry you…?'

Now he looked wary. 'Yes…and I meant it. If that's what it takes to prove to you that—'

Lia put a finger over his lips, stopping him. She felt suddenly unsure, but forged on. 'The thing is…I appreciate that…but I'm just…that is, I'm just wondering…if you didn't feel you had to do that would you *want* to marry me?'

A look that Lia couldn't decipher came into Ben's eyes and then he was putting his hands on her arms and pushing her away from him so he could slip out of the bed. Lia sat up, feeling cold, not liking the insecurity she felt. Maybe it was too soon…

Gloriously naked, Ben was rummaging around in his pockets for something, and then he came back to the bed. He knelt in front of her and she pulled the sheet up over her chest.

He held a black box in his hands. Velvet. She looked from it to him, her throat going dry.

He said carefully, 'I didn't show this to you because I didn't want to push you.'

He opened the box then, and Lia looked down, eyes widening. Nestled against black silk was the most beautiful ring she'd ever seen. A rectangular-shaped sapphire flanked by rows of diamonds.

'The thing is,' Ben said, sounding uncharacteristically nervous, 'if you don't like it we can change it. But I'd like to ask if you'd accept this ring and consent to be my fiancée—for as long as you like. And if you ever decide you'd like to get married, then I'll be waiting.'

Lia felt emotion rise up to squeeze her throat.

Happiness fizzed through her veins. And something else. A sense of freedom from the weight of the past.

She looked at Ben but he was blurry through her tears. She said, half-crying, half-laughing, 'I love it—and, *yes*. I accept. Now. I'll marry you, Ben Carter, if you'll have me.'

He looked at her for a long moment, stunned, and then Lia threw her arms around him, tumbling their two naked bodies back onto the bed, limbs entwining.

She was soon sprawled over his chest and Ben took her left hand. He looked at her as he pushed the ring down onto her finger, saying huskily, 'I love you, Julianna Ford.'

The ring nestled on her finger, fitting like a glove, and she wrapped her arms around his neck, love cracking her wide open. 'I love you too, Benjamin Carter...now, where were we?'

EPILOGUE

'The team are on the ground in India now, Lia. We can't thank you enough for what you're doing. You and Ben. Your charity has been invaluable in restoring order to the chaos.'

Lia looked out of the window of her office. 'I'm just sorry I can't be with you all at the moment.'

The man on the other end of the phone huffed a chuckle. 'Don't worry—your expertise is invaluable even from there, and I don't think that husband of yours will be letting you out of his sight any time soon.'

Lia's hand automatically went to her distended belly, and she glanced through the glass wall separating her office from her husband's in his London building, where they were now based.

Ben had agreed to relocate to the UK so that they could be near her father, who appeared to be undergoing a renaissance since Ben and he had merged companies, turning them into a formidable transatlantic company called CarterFord Construction. Her father had taken a long-overdue step back and was currently on a cruise with his new love—his long-serving secretary. For years Lia had suspected her of being in love with her father. They were very sweet together.

She frowned when she couldn't see her husband in his office and sat up straight, saying distractedly, 'Okay, Philip, please keep us updated on the development anyway.'

Lia put down the phone and stood up—and then smiled when she realised why he hadn't been able to see her husband. She went out of her office and into his, leaning on the doorframe, her hand on her eight months pregnant belly.

Ben looked up at her from his vantage point sprawled on the floor, shirtsleeves rolled up and hair mussed. His eyes gleamed and he put a finger to his mouth.

Their three-year-old daughter, Lucy, hadn't seen Lia yet, and she was saying in a very familiar authoritative voice, '*No*, Daddy—see? We have to build a room for the fire truck 'n all the animals.'

Fierce love and joy bloomed inside Lia— so much so it nearly took her breath away. She blinked away sudden tears, cursing her pregnancy hormones.

Ben sat up and reached a hand up to her, and then Lucy turned around and squealed excitedly, 'Mummy! Come see what we're making!'

Lia came in and knelt on the ground carefully, mindful of her extra cargo, and Ben pulled her into his embrace, his arms wrapping possessively around her belly.

Lucy, a dark-haired, blue-eyed imp who kept them very busy, jumped up. 'Can I listen to my little brother?'

Ben and Lia opened their arms and Lucy nestled in close to Lia's belly, face turned to one side, brow etched with fierce concentration, her little arms spread out to encompass Lia's expanded waist.

Lia leaned back into Ben's broad chest and felt him pull her hair to one side so he could kiss her neck. She shivered deliciously, and just then the baby kicked. Lucy giggled.

Lia felt Ben's smile against her skin and smiled in response.

He spoke against her neck. *'I love you...'*
And she turned her head and whispered back.
'I love you too...'

* * * * *

The BRIDES FOR BILLIONAIRES *series*
continues with
MARRIED FOR THE ITALIAN'S HEIR
by Rachael Thomas
Available March 2017

If you enjoyed this story, check out
these other great reads from Abby Green
AWAKENED BY HER DESERT CAPTOR
AN HEIR FIT FOR A KING
THE BRIDE FONSECA NEEDS
FONSECA'S FURY
Available now!